Published in 2022 by Exhale Publishing
Copyright © Careen Latoya Lawrence

Exhale Publishing is part of 4D-House Ltd.

Exhale Publishing   **4D HOUSE**

Prepared for publishing by Careen Latoya Lawrence
Cover Design: Careen Latoya Lawrence

A CIP catalogue record for this title is available from the British Library.

ISBN: 978-1-3999-4852-4

Letters In Black

CAREEN LATOYA LAWRENCE

Exhale Publishing

Letters in Black

CAREEN LATOYA LAWRENCE

Trigger Warning:

This book is centred around child sexual abuse and insest, not only experienced by female characters. Additionally, there are descriptions of domestic violence.

By no means is this book written to glorify child sexual abuse or incest, domestic or any other abuse. Instead, it is to highlight the unspoken cases, situations we know happen, but are quiet about. This book is to shed light on these events in hope that you, as readers, will take in consideration the Black man when the discussion of 'protecting Black women' pops up around you.

As we progress as humans, as a people, as Black people, I hope we will begin to not only protect our Black girls, but we will also protect our Black boys before it's too late.

'Secrets keep you sick.'
Incest Survivor Interview – Star
Soft White Underbelly on YouTube

Dear Black Man,

You with strength
Mountain of passion
Definition of life to be lived.
You, with joy behind lids
Let light shine like the sun.
You are son.
Placing an emphasis on mother's lessons.
You, be great,
With heart being shared.
And your art,
Your art is an air of fresh.
Your art unscathed, trades honesty
Packs punches
Leaves holes in the guilty,
They who the shoe fits,
The Cinderellas of life.
You are unbothered by the way they feel
And there is everything right with that.
You know who you are,
You seek no validation.
That is your super power Black Man.
If they can't match that,
Let them wallow in their lies.
You, keep growing
You, keep healing
You, keep being honest with self.
I see you Black Man.

Love,
A Black Woman

Dedication:

To the Black men around the world who have been sexually assaulted and the Black men in my life who have been silenced or ever felt they needed to be silent.

I love you.

Tuesday, 24 May

Dear Black Man,

Beautiful Black King, how are you today? Like, how are you really? How was your day? Have you managed to overcome any fears today? I love you Black man.   5:32 am

Wednesday, 25 May

Dear Black Man,

I know you've had some losses so I just want to let you know, you are in my prayers. To lose loved ones isn't easy, so rest assured, you have someone praying for you. Keep your strength in God, even if you can't find comfort in anyone on Earth. Know that He's got open arms for you, His son.

I love you Black man.   5:32 am

Thursday, 26 May

Dear Black Man,

When you are able to, take some time out to reconnect with nature. There is magic to be found in the Earth. You just need to be still enough to be able to accept it. In the midst of your trials, your spirit will appreciate the time to renew your inner powers.

I love you Black man.   5:32 am

Friday, 27 May

Dear Black Man,

I miss hearing the huskiness of your voice. My face
misses the smiles you're able to bring to it. I do
hope you are well.

Love you Black Man.   5:32 am

Saturday, 28 May

Dear Black Man,

I want you to believe in how powerful you are.
I want you to take some time to evaluate your
journey thus far, for within it, I hope you find your
power.

I love you Black man.   5:32 am

Sunday, 29 May

Dear Black Man,

There are times I want to be angry at you. Like
today for instance. I know you're going through it,
but, I just want to talk to you, hear you laugh once
more. I just want to feel the warmth in your voice,
and see the comfort in your eyes. I want to be angry
and I know it's selfish of me. Please forgive me. I
understand how important this is for you.

I love you Black man.   5:32 am

Monday, 30 May

Dear Black Man,
I tell you I love you because I do love you,
because it's the right thing to say. You deserve

<S shayla

to know that you are loved. I want your world to
revolve around love. It is your birth right.

Love you Black Man.   5:32 am

He found himself back in a place where replying to her messages felt
impossible. He read them all, over and over before being able to accept
her kind words. He hated this time of year and couldn't face himself
nor his reality. He still managed to make it to work, but his routine was
as broken as his spirit was.

He would have loved to reply to her messages, but, couldn't. Not
yet. To comprehend her love, her honesty, her wants for him, it was not
something he was able to do. He was eternally grateful to have her in
his life and he could not have asked for a better woman.

The way she supported him, it's as though she was with him from
the beginning and it felt that way. There was never any judgement
dripping from her voice, or clinging to her texts, or creeping in her
eyes. She simply allowed him to live, allowed him to breathe, allowed
him to be.

To him, she was an angel God bestowed upon his life and even that
was beyond what his mind would allow him to believe; he was deserv-
ing of her as a gift to him. There was something about her which would
pull him off the cliff he so frequently visited. *What she doesn't know
won't hurt,* was a mantra to him over the past two years, yet guilt would
not allow him to go through with it. Seeing himself daily, served as his
own trigger warning.

118 Elm Tree Road
Lewisham
England
SE13 5SQ
31st May 2019

Glen,

     I can't even lie, I'm happy to hear you passed away. It sounds harsh to say 'died', but 'transition' is too peaceful for the likes of you. The life you subjected others to was wicked. I don't know how you got away with it for so many years, but I'm happy you lived out the rest of your life behind bars.

     You don't even know how much you messed up everyone around you. Me. Chloe. Those who came forward at your trial. You put a cloud over our heads. Some may say it's wrong for me to think this, but out of everyone you poisoned, I think I'm the one who was worst impacted. Just because you were locked away, it don't mean you were the only one behind bars.

     It was always painful when I'd think about everything from back in the day. Now I think about it, if you were never been turned in, if there was never a court case, Avery would have been okay to this day.

     I don't know how to explain it, but it's not even like I wanted to. I just felt like that little boy again. I could hear your voice in my head, goading me on. Just like when Chloe and I were at your place. You used to say 'Ricky, man nuh fi fraid ah pussy. Touch it nuh man.' I heard you. I was only a boy then, but you forced me into a perverted manhood.

     I tried talking to my parents 'bout it, but, they forced me to pretend that nothing happened. The people who were to protect me, forced me to lock away all of my emotions, my fears, the abuse. If only I could go back in time, I'd force them to listen. Not like that would work through. My dad was devil.

     One minute, when we have guests, he's 'the man', but as soon as we had no audience for him to fool, he'd switch. My mum was always the recipient of his abuse, physical, verbal and emotional.

I grew up in purgatory but lived in hell.

How could you have done what you did to your niece and nephew? You were meant to look after us, not abuse us. I don't even know if I would have preferred exchanging the type of abuse I went through. I needed to be loved man. I needed an adult to teach me about love.

A lot of my habits came from not being loved. Take my cousin Niyah, I started touching her when she was 7. I hated her because our grandparents loved her openly. What I learned from you, I used to hurt her, to manipulate her into thinking I would like her. I was jealous of her. She had adults who loved her. I had adults who taught me nothing about love. What you did to me, turned me into a monster.

I'm glad you're dead. If only I could right my wrongs, things would be better. Instead, I'm writing to you. My dead uncle.

Ricky.

Tuesday, 31 May

Dear Black Man,

I see the pains you wear on your body. I can tell
that you fight with the demons of your traumas.
You speak with strength but I feel as though
you're in need of care.

Black Man, I'm here for you, be open with me. I
want you to survive. You are loved. I see everything
you've tried to hide. Believe me, you are worthy.

Love you Black Man.

5:32 am

118 Elm Tree Road
Lewisham
England
SE13 5SQ
31st May 2022

Yo Shayla!

Thanks for your message Queen, I needed it. It was a blessing to read first thing in the morning. Swear you know when my alarm was gonna go off. Came just in time. I don't usually check my phone in the mornings, but glad I did today.

My brother showed up at mine recently trying to persuade me to attend a memorial for our uncle. Today is the two-year anniversary of his death and these lot think it's a good idea to celebrate a man who spent time in jail for sexual assault. This man had no remorse for what he did. I can't find it in myself to show up for him.

Another reason I can't attend is because of my niece. You remember Avery, David's little girl? Well, she's not so little anymore. I can't, with everything that's happened, I can't attend any family function if I know she will be there. She's been through enough already you know.

David's my brother and I love him, but I couldn't see eye to eye with him when he came over. This man disregarded the wellbeing of his child like it was nothing. It was too easy for him. The way he brushed everything aside was mad. I expected more from him to be honest and that's probably what the problem was you know. I get that it's good to be around family and all that, but, when you've been me, and you've done some shit, the best thing for you to do, is to stay away.

Man really tried to guilt trip me. My brother looked me dead in the eyes and said 'why is it a problem to you? You're my brother and we didn't press charges. There's no restraining order against you. It was six years ago, she don't remember what happened.' Shay, how can a father say something like that? How can a father dismiss his child's wellbeing like that? It don't make sense Queen.

To see the cycle continue is honestly painful. David, just like our parents placed no value on the mental welfare of his child. I don't think it's fair to say it's a Black thing, but from some of the conversations I've had, Black families are guilty of this.

What is it about Black families that stops them from listening to their children? What is it that stops them from protecting their children? Why is there such a failure in seeing the importance of our children, and how a cycle of trauma may cause them to inflict what they've seen on others? I know this from experience. I've been that child.

I won't even hold you much longer. But know this, I appreciate you. Thanks for being around for me. To have you in my corner means a lot.

Love and Peace,

Ricardo.

Chapter 1: **RELATIONSHIPS**

Monday, 6 June

Dear Black Man,

Relationships aren't easy, but it doesn't mean you
should give up when things get rough. This
applies not only to romantic relationships, but to
friendships and your relationship with family
members also.

If there are frayed bonds you wish to mend, if you
think the relationship can be salvaged, reach out.

Love you.

5:32 am

"I guess nothing's changed. I grew up in a house where I was only seen when in trouble, only heard when crying but immediately forced into silence. To be a child with no identity, or at least, a child with a false identity was detrimental for me then, and now. It makes you creative, you know. You have to find other ways to express yourself." Ricardo paused as he looked around his surroundings. He managed to compose himself as best as possible. He needed to be able to get through all he had to say to her.

"I wrote a letter to my uncle when I found out he died because of an email I got from my cousin Chloe. Have you ever suppressed memories for so long, they give you a headache when it comes crashing in? No shit, it's not something I would wish on my worst enemy." He was nervous, she could tell from the way his words flew from his lips.

Looking into her eyes he saw something he hadn't expected, love. After everything, she still loved him. This was by far the most unexpected thing for him.

"Who is Chloe? Tell me about her." She interrupted his stream of thoughts.

Who was Chloe, he thought. He looked past her as though Chloe had appeared to remind him about who she was.

"She is the only cousin I ever connected with when growing up. Our relationship was better than what I had with my own brother." Allowing a smile to form across his lips, he allowed the memory of her to fill his mind. "Chloe was the one who taught me how to do handstands. She used to beat me up too. We took Tae-kwon-do when we were kids and she used to beat me up."

"The devil is a liar." She laughed. "You were training? You? You were training to be Blackie-Chan? How did I never know this?"

"Wrong art form for Blackie-Chan, but yeah, I was about that life."

If there was a sliver of time he would have wanted to hold onto a lot longer, this was it. To be able to share space and time, to allow her the opportunity to know him, was more than he could have asked for. He's not had much opportunity to tell his story, to explain himself, so this was important. It was a milestone.

Had it not been for Shayla's text two weeks ago, as well as him being inebriated, this moment would have never happened. Liquid courage was one hell of a thing. Without alcohol, there would be no push to send a DM begging to talk, along with how sorry and how stupid he was.

Ricardo had never, before meeting Shayla, despite being in relationships, disclosed his true feelings. Some would say this is attributed to his past, causing him to distrust those around him, coupled with the inability to form bonds with those he was romantically involved with. Ricardo on the other hand, in the past, knowing nothing about introspection, saw himself as broken and called himself a prick for failing at relationships.

§§§

Embarrassment crawled over his skin like tattoos being etched onto his body, when he woke from his nap. Ricardo was never one to believe that Black people could blush, but, to see her staring at him, smiling, he felt his cheeks burning, as described in books, or from White people he'd overheard.

The train came to a halt at Canada Water, freeing up seats for commuters impatiently waiting to board. The gentleman who had been wrestling with a sleeping Ricardo for the armrest made his move to leave his seat. It seems as though Shayla had been waiting for some time for the seat to become vacant so she could swoop in. It took her a split second to fill the gap created by her fellow commuter.

"Hey, may I have a look at the blurb of your book please?"

"Yeah, sure." He handed her the book, shocked at how proper she spoke.

Definitely not from South, he thought. No South London female speaks as well as her. In fact, no Black woman from South talks that way.

"Looks good. How far are you with it?" She asked, thumbing the book's jacket before returning it.

"It's decent." He responded. "I'm not as far as I would have loved to be, but, it's alright so far."

Commuters hovered above the strangers sitting in awkwardness hoping the air would suffocate one in good time. The rustle of the train over metal tracks played a faint soundtrack in the background accompanied by lyrics written from the voices of drunken passengers carrying the melody of their conversation's silence.

The break in their conversation came to an end with Shayla asking "self-help books your usual go to?"

He noticed the small smile which caused her lip to curl. "What you saying? A Black man can't read self-help books?" He chuckled.

"He can-"

"But?"

"Just never thought I'd see a Black man clutching so tightly to his self-help book on the train."

"You've probably never looked closely enough," he chuckled lightly as his tongue hopped over words that would come across as rude.

Shayla had never seen a Black man, in public, with a self-help book. It made her pleased to witness this as she had always hoped that men, particularly Black men, would begin to show that they have the ability to do the work needed for themselves.

"Where are you getting off?" Shayla asked, noticing Ricardo looking up at the running display. "If you've got enough time, do you mind telling me about what got you into self-help books?"

"I'll see what I can tell you in two stops." He said with nonchalance.

"Swear? I'm getting off at Sydenham as well. You just can't seem to get rid of me, can you?"

Something in her boldness comforted Ricardo. Their conversation continued for the rest of their journey and, to their surprise, continued for another 20 minutes as they walked side by side in the cool of the night. Those 20 minutes, filled with laughter, would lend themselves to years to come, which neither party could see.

§§§

Though 2019 seemed far away in history, Ricardo has cherished the friendship he was able to build with Shayla. He was thankful to her that he was now better able to understand himself and the importance of healing.

"So, be real with me, other than being drunk, why did you message me?"

Sitting back in his chair, he exhaled like never before. He knew this question was coming, but no matter how much he tried to rehearse a response, he found himself struggling. He knew she wasn't stupid, so would have known there was more to his message.

"It's been almost two years, and you disappeared even though the police let you go and there were no charges against you." She calmly strung her words together taking a sip of her now cold coffee.

"A friend of mine sent me a text one morning which hit hard. It was on my head from that day, then, after drinking heavy like a fool, I had the courage to message you I guess."

The chatter around them seemed to have grown louder. The hiss of steam from the machines craved attention from baristas. The smell of paninis uttered their need to enter into the space along with the fragrance of freshly brewed coffee. Ricardo's senses were heightened the second his response leapt from his lips.

She tried to analyse him, searching for clues about his sincerity in the moment. His body language was difficult to be read. She believed that he was being honest with her. There was no reason for any feigned words, at least, none that she could think of. He's been one of the 'ghost' family members for years now, and she couldn't think of reasons as to why he would pop up now under false pretences.

Ricardo failed to let her know he had written a letter to her that very morning, during his sobriety. This letter was sitting in his pocket burning a very painful hole into his leg, screaming to be released.

The only word she was able to summon in that moment was 'seen' which was followed by an unprecedented, heavy silence.

< S shayla

Monday, 6 June

Dear Black Man,

I can't get over how handsome you are. I've stared at my phone's screen so many times just asking, why you are as attractive as you are. I love seeing your smile. I just wish there was more of it.

A man as attractive, as handsome as you, needs to know, just because you've experienced hard times, times you're unable to talk about, they do not make you less than anyone.

Love you Black Man.

7:52 pm

118 Elm Tree Road
Lewisham
England
SE13 5SQ
31st May 2022

Man like Ricky,

I wish you would have had Shayla in your life from back in the day. Since she's popped up, I've been feeling better about a lot of things, and that person you and I were, she's helped me to get to know and understand him so much better.

A lesson I've cherished is this, though I did some uncharacteristic things as a youth, some were a result of learnt behaviour. Neither you, nor I, had the best individuals to guide us. We were given Glen as an uncle, and that man wasn't for us. Our growth was forced so we became 'a man' before we were able to embrace our youth, our childhood. Our father wasn't the greatest role model either, not after everything he put us through. I'm not excusing the behaviour, I'm simply saying, if we had better around, maybe the outcome would have been different. You aren't a monster, nor am I. I know there are guys who would have loved to have a male figure in their lives, there's nothing wrong with that, my thing is, how can you appreciate what was there though it didn't serve you well?

That being said, there is so much expected from Black men nowadays, yet, only few are able to acknowledge that some of these expectations are bullshit. Black men who aren't around for their kids get so much cussing, but people don't even realise that some of these men were never taught HOW to be there fully. I'm not even speaking for the men who walked out for no good reason. The men who came from good homes. I'm talking about the men who didn't have another man to teach them. The ones whose fathers were absent. Even if they had a father like ours, they were still not role models. These men were worse than the fathers who were never around.

How is it that anyone can expect men who had no true role models, no true teachers to be exemplary fathers?

Another frustrating expectation, is that Black men are to love Black women fully. Again, don't get me wrong, there's nothing wrong with wanting our Black women to be truly loved, not fetishised or to be kept as trophy wives, but to truly be loved. However, going back to not having role models to teach these things, how is this even an expectation? How is it even fair to dismiss the men who don't know how to love Black women? There are Black men out there who CHOOSE to disrespect Black women and you can even see that from how they treat their mothers, but for guys like us, like me, I know I have work to do to be able to love Black women as they are to be loved.

Before I even talk about guys like us, let me just address the guys who truly make it bad for us. The Black men who had the role models, the fathers they would call simps, these men will not call their mothers because she may have said something they weren't keen on. Maybe they even felt that punishments they received as kids was too harsh, these men who start disrespecting their mothers, they are the ones who are meant to be blackballed. These kinds of guys probably have deeper issues than what they learnt at home, but, they were taught.

As for guys like us, what people tend to forget is that it was important for us to learn key lessons as kids. For a child to know anything, particularly in their primitive stage of development, it needs to be taught. These lessons happen naturally from behaviours seen, or from parents explicitly, intentionally telling them or showing them. Now, if me as a little boy, from an uncle or father, was never shown how to treat a Black woman with care, is it right for the rest of the Black community to criticise me as a man? It's taken too many years for me to understand how imperative it was to have been taught how to treat women.

Had Glen not been the man he was, I would have never manipulated Niyah. The woman she is today, would have never had scars upon her psyche had I known how special she was. My insecurities would have never overpowered me into believing she was to be improperly treated. My hands would have never explored her.

Honestly, Shayla has been a blessing to me. Had you met her, the woman she is today, things would have never happened with Avery. I'm bold in saying that, but I guess that's solely if you had been opened to changing who you were then. I know you had no intention of harming Avery, but, it happened, and it shouldn't have. Shayla teaches love in a way I can't explain, which is why I'm certain you would have benefitted from her. There is so much you could have learned from her back then.

As for Tamara, I don't think I would have ever gotten involved with her. She was special, nah, she is special. There was a light in her, and like a moth, I was attracted. That's all I was though, a moth, not even a real man. She deserved a whole lot more, so if I knew Shayla from before, I would have done Tamara the honour of staying out of her life.

I tried a thing, wasn't good enough though.
Wish me well. I'm going to close this off here.

Love,

Your Present Self.

P.s. we will come back to loving Black women, that's key.

Chapter 2: **MONSTER**

< S shayla

Dear Black Man,

I want you to remember that you are no monster.
Life threw adversities your way, starving you of love
but this does not make you a monster.

I love you and believe in you. I need you to believe
in yourself also. Without your belief, it means nothing.
I want you to seek help. Find someone who will help
you to safely navigate through your history.

Work through the pain and the joy on the other side
will be more than you can imagine right now.

I love you Black Man.   5:32 am

"I need to start charging you for these sessions." She joked. The irony in her words caused both to laugh.

"Fam, if that's what it will take, I'm here for it." Ricardo knew it must have been difficult for her to utter such words as the past, though distant, was still a new memory. Nevertheless, this wasn't something he would pass up. Slightly dipping his head to the left, eyebrows raised and a questioning left hand, he looked at her awaiting a response.

This was the second time in less than a week that they've seen each other. Sharing space and time with her meant the world to him. He felt as though she had forgiven him, a lesson he would be able to cherish, having never been able to do this. At least, he hoped that this was her showing that she had pardoned him, or was working on it.

Three years ago, he attempted to get the attention of his cousin in the hopes they would talk. He wanted to apologies for his misconduct as a child, nevertheless, his actions, his choice, the way he figured best to handle things, led to his misfortune, which some may say was self-inflicted.

Caffe Nero seemed to be captivated by individuals wishing for conversation today. Ricardo observed silence dancing on table tops. Looking at the coffee lovers around, he saw their hopes to speak. He saw how they fought the urge to communicate, wishing they hadn't sworn to have a moment's silence on his behalf, allowing the opportunity to sift through the stinging roars of self-doubt which threatened to cloud his judgement.

It's as though she could sense everything he was trying to wish away, she reached out, gently placing her hand on his forearm. She wanted to tell him that he had nothing to worry about, and that she had completely forgiven him for everything. However, she wasn't entirely sure that this was true and instead asked "what's troubling you?"

The truth managed to seal itself on the tip of his tongue, and as if on cue, perfectly orchestrated and prompted by a conductor, the buzz in Nero resumed. No-one held on to sympathy for him any longer.

"Don't worry, let's order." She rushed to say as they stepped closer to the till. Looking closely at his face, as a stranger, she was able to see behind the façade he was attempting to wear. She saw the pill he was swallowing, faking the notion that he was ready for this conversation.

"Aight." He felt his heart rate suddenly decrease. He hadn't noticed how erratic it had been beating before those four words from her. He smiled, "I'll cover it."

"Hiya, have in or takeaway." The barista, a petite black woman, interrupted. Her accent gave her away telling that she wasn't originally from the UK. Her features were strong enough to make you believe she was Eritrean or Ethiopian. Ricardo always had difficulties telling them apart. Her eyes, perfectly oval, her face with a beautiful length, and her hair, with its loose curls, set her apart from others.

"Have in please." He replied, admiring her beauty and taking in the reassurance from the barista's smile as she patiently waited to take their order. Looking to his companion, he stepped aside allowing her the opportunity to order first.

"I'll have a large hazelnut oat mocha, single shot coffee please and no cream."

"That's a, single shot, oat mocha, hazelnut syrup and was that a large with cream?" The barista had been repeating while entering it into the till.

"Yes, large, but no cream."

"Oh sorry. Thank you." She punched in. "Is that all for you?"

"Err, a slice of cheesecake as well please." She chuckled, placing a finger to her nose, slightly bowing her head.

"Problems for no reason-" Ricardo added causing those in earshot to laugh.

The barista smiled, "and for you sir?"

"Just a large Americano for me thanks."

The variance of skin complexions within the diaspora was incomparable Ricardo thought as they stepped aside awaiting their order. There was a calm which fell between them holding some discomfort, bombarding Ricardo with where and how to begin. She was also struggling with how she truly felt. Neither of the two were sure as to whether today would work according to their plans.

Ricardo knew they had a difficult topic ahead to be discussed; she knew she would need to say something, and he knew it was coming.

He rubbed his hand over his face, a perfectly chiselled jawline, no chinstrap, and no beard to hide his features. His lips were accentuated by his moustache, his nose, wide with a broad bridge. His piercing eyes were juxtaposed by the warmth and welcoming brown of his iris; they were bold. His melanin provided his skin with riches of Black gold, perfected by the dark oceanic waves a top his head, outlined by the mid fade he sported.

Ricardo exhaled sharply, scrunching his lips as he chewed on his thoughts. After meeting with her two days ago, he figured this meet up would have also gone smoothly.

She felt as though she was outside her body, floating about them, with her thoughts on display. She would have given anything for today to have gone as smoothly as Sunday did. As she watched her spirit floating between them, she could feel the heaviness in her chest with each breath she took.

Both equally battled with this phase of healing. It was an unexpected shift. A plot twist if you may. How could it be, for her who already ventured into her healing, to struggle to speak, and for him who had just begun, to find himself here, so quickly?

"When's the last time you spoke to Chloe?" She broke into the silence clinging to her words for dear life.

When is the last time? He asked himself. Does communicating with dishonesty as your director count?

§§§

from: Chloe Bennett <chloeb@bennettsinterior.co.uk>
to: Ricardo Bennett <r.bennett@gmail.com>
date: 31 May 2019, 18:57
subject: Hey cuz

I don't even know where to begin, 'hi' could possibly suffice but I've been MIA for years, so I don't think it's enough. I don't know what is good enough as a hello, but it's all I can think of right now, hi.

It's probably wrong of me to pop up now, but, I had never wanted to return, so long as he was alive. I know it's crazy because he's been away for a while, but I couldn't bring myself to it you know.

The first thing I said when I heard about his death was 'glad di bitch dead'. I felt so relieved. A huge weight fell from my body. As an uncle, he took advantage of his role and his power as an adult. I'm happy my parents listened when I told them about what he was up to. Saying that, I'm sorry your parents weren't supportive with everything. I only found this out recently when talking to my mum. I honestly don't remember what the conversation was initially about. All I remember was it being about two weeks before his death and as I sat with my parents, I was wishing that the man would drop dead, boof.

I still feel sick to the core when I think about what he'd say to you about me, and what he had you do to me. How is it that a man who was an uncle to so many, who was to be trusted, turn out the way he did? As an uncle, he missed all the marks. If he was that way with us, only God knows what he did to kids that weren't his relatives. I want to believe that he was the victim to someone else's sick twisted mind when he was a child. Maybe then I could forgive him but right now I can't excuse him any of what he done. I'd never excuse him.

Some of the things this man used to say to me stayed with me for so long. Up to this day I've not told my parents about it. I don't think it would even make a difference to them, or to me, but it ate away at me for years. I thought I was able to master healing, but everything had a tight hold on me to this day.

Ricky, I cried. For the first time in 30 years, I cried. I bawled my eyes out. It was so hard to hear that this devil of a man died without doing enough time for his wrongs. I don't think I can go to his funeral though because I honestly think I will spit on his grave.

Well, this email took an unexpected turn. Sorry to have laden you with this. Seems like I had more trapped within me than I realised.

Hope to hear back from you though. I hope you've been well and looking after yourself. One day I'd love to meet up with you, probably not in Blue Borough, is it still called that? But yeah, anywhere that's not Lewisham Borough is good for me.

Love cuz.

Chloe.

Letters in Black

from: Ricardo Bennett <r.bennett@gmail.com>
to: Chloe Bennett <chloeb@bennettsinterior.co.uk>
date: 31 May 2019, 22:33
subject: Re: Hey cuz

Bennett's Interior yeah? Proud of you twin. Don't even worry 'bout the 'hi' thing. I'll hold it against you next time. Hearing from you made my day. It's been time!

I get you on the whole thing about being happy he died. He should have kick the bucket from time! Why he breathed so long is out of my remit to know, but, he's gone now, that's all that counts. Di dutty dawg dead an gone! I hope God don't strike us for speaking ill against the dead still.

Anyway cuz, it was good to hear from you. I'm gonna head off to bed now.

How's the interior design life treating you?

Stay bless.
Ricky.

Drafts

from: Ricardo Bennett <r.bennett@gmail.com>
to: Chloe Bennett <chloeb@bennettsinterior.co.uk>
subject: Re: Hey cuz

It's been a lot of years forreal. Don't even worry about the 'hi' situation, I'll hold it against you next time lol.

I get what you mean about not wanting to have come back while he was still breathing. He put us through a lot. I don't know how I even managed to, but I visited him one time. Man was happy that I went to see him. He was sick and I don't mean, a physical thing, I actually mean, the man needed to see a therapist kind of sick.

He looked so old, like, prison really aged him. He had forehead lines that were so pronounced and frown lines between his brows. His eyes were tired. You could see the formation of mouth frown, and he lost a lot of weight. When he saw me, his eyes lit up and his first words were 'Ricky! Good fi si yuh mi favaret nephew'. His favourite nephew you know? I challenged him on it, like, how was I your favourite when you put me through shit? Man looked at me like I was mad and told me that he didn't know what I was talking about. He claimed he never put me through shit and all he did was teach me how to be a man. How did he think he was teaching me to be a man by telling me shit like man aint meant to be scared of pussy and made me feel like I needed to overpower women through manipulation?

I wanna believe that he was raised the way he got us to interact, but part of me thinks he was really just a dutty dawg. I don't think you've heard, I'm sure if you did your email would have been different, but, I almost became just like him, sitting in prison, aging faster than the days would go by. David's got a daughter, Avery, I was babysitting her one day, she was 10 at the time, something came over me, I don't know how to explain it, but, one minute we were sitting there watching a movie, I moved closer to her, then told her to sit on my lap. To this day I can't believe I did that to her, I told her to sit on my lap and she did. She was scared of me. I was a monster. I was a piece of shit. She was wearing a blue skirt and she sat on my lap. Her body stiffened as the piece of shit I was, put my hand up her skirt. As dirty as I feel now I think about it, I'm happy David and his wife, Eva, walked in when they did because I don't even want to know what I would have done next. They saved Avery from me and saved me from myself that day.

I get it if you think I should be stoned to death. I get it if you hate me after this, but I had to be honest, you know.

I'm happy your parents removed you from the situation. That's what a good parent should do. They took you away so you didn't have to endure it any longer. Sad to say, my parents kept sending me back, more my dad than my mum. My mum complied to save herself. Had she dared to disagree, the consequences would be more than she'd have asked for. There were days she couldn't go to work because no amount of makeup would hide the bruises. I wish she would have packed up her stuff and ours and walked out on my dad. She had ample opportunity, but I think she was shook. David was the one who would snitch on her sometimes if she did something out of line or if she disciplined him and he knew dad would have probably said something different.

I know I'm a monster for what I did to his daughter, but that man dances with the devil and paves the way for the devil to walk. Imagine after everything with Avery, this man would invite me into his home. I used to hear his wife in the background yelling 'if you make that man come near me and my child, I will kill you both.' I don't blame her. Any good parent would want to save their child from sitting in the same room, same house, as their abuser, but, not all parents are the same I guess.

§§§

"So?" She pressed.

"Huh?" He shook his head as though trying to erase his flashback.

"Chloe, when's the last time you spoke to her?"

"Well, that's the thing, we haven't spoken in a while, but we've been emailing, it's sporadic, but we've been emailing."

"That's good." She bit the inside of her bottom lip. She knew what she needed to ask, she knew where this conversation was to go, but forcing herself to steer it there was another fight.

Ricardo did to her the thing which caused her to doubt herself. The thing which led to her being pregnant. The thing which led to her being in the hospital. The thing which led to her first miscarriage. Her chest now heavy with worry, she finished her coffee, her cheesecake still sitting on the table untouched, and sighed heavily.

"I don't think I can stay for long today." She stared at the table twiddling her thumbs.

"I'm sorry." Ricardo managed to muster while looking at her, hoping she would look at him and see the truth in his eyes.

"Huh?" She responded slowly lifting her head.

"I'm sorry. I know I did some things which caused you to not trust me and honestly, I'm sorry. Not that it can take away whatever pains I caused, but I-"

"It's cool. Don't even worry about it." She started.

"Nah it's not though Niyah. I was a dickhead and am coming to terms with it."

"You were young. I forgive you. I forgave you a while back-"

Unsure if he was to press the issue any further, he sat back in his chair and stared into his cup. He couldn't understand how she could have possibly forgiven him, what he did was punishable. Two days ago, he hoped for forgiveness, today hearing the words escape her lips, he couldn't comprehend it. He was also unable to understand how it was that he was never punished for his misdemeanour.

Niyah wanted to believe that she had forgiven him, but her spirit felt unsettled, there was a cloud of uncertainty surrounding her. She wanted to push her chair back, rise to her feet and walk away, but she was unable to will herself to move. The couple sitting two tables to the left of them chatted away, well, one did the talking, telling a story in a very animated manner, and the other listened, nodding when she felt it was the right time to show she was still engaged. The clattering of cutleries being put aside to be washed, the hissing of the coffee machine, the chatter of their neighbours, the music which seeped through the speakers above all seemed to grow as the two slipped into an uncharacteristic silence.

< S shayla

Dear Black Man,

You are a King. I know you've got a lot going on.
You've been working so hard and at times it seems
you're putting out all that energy in vain, but rest
assured, it's not all for nothing.

Everything you've asked for is on its way to you. Be
patient. Be kind to yourself. Love yourself. Be your
best self. I love you Black man.

21:47pm

Chapter 3: **HEALING**

Wednesday, 8 June

Dear Black Man,

Have I ever told you that I love you purely? Do you understand what that means? To be loved purely that is.

My pure love for you comes without condition. It means I have no expectations hanging above your head. It means I want what's best for you. A pure love doesn't judge, it only wishes to understand what's going on and what led you to be who you are today. I love you.   5:32am

Yo Shayla

Thanks for the text Queen. I know I've been distant lately and I apologise. It's that time again where the past floods in and leaves me in the worst way. I'll drop you a call one day.

5:50am   Love Queen.

eh, it's nothing. Hope you've been keeping well. Eating, staying hydrated, sleeping, creaming your skin. That type of stuff.   5:51am

:laughing emoji: creaming my skin every day. How've you been?
5:55am

So creaming your skin is all you've been doing? How about eating? Staying hydrated? Sleeping?

I've been better. Getting over a dumb ass cold though. Imagine people have been staring at me hard because I've been coughing? See how Covid have people acting like say regular colds never existed! Kmt   5:57am

Ha! What's a regular cold though? Dem tings don't exist again man. You either have Covid or you're well haha. Hope you get back to 100 soon Queen.

5:57am

Thanks King. I hope so too. The way you so conveniently skipped out on answering my question makes me think that you've not fully been looking after yourself, so I'm just going to say I hope you'll be able to have some full on self-care moments. Take your time to heal King.

6:03am

HEAL. How does someone heal when their wounds are not physical? When they can't be seen, not by naked eyes. When they can't be seen by x-rays. When they can't be seen by endoscope cameras. How does someone heal when their wounds are caused by years of abuse? When their wounds date back to witnessing ordeals which should never have happened in the first place, how do they heal?

Ricardo understood healing in the physical sense, but this was on a different level. To Ricardo, it was metaphysical. He knew what she meant though, he needed to heal from his traumas.

Ricardo chuckled as he reread Shayla's last text. It's ironic he thought. This journey he was on, started in 2019, after a death. Healing, in the physical sense occurs after an injury. And here he was, healing after a death, three years later. Had he ever been looking for a joke, this was it, albeit with a very dry wit.

Standing by his window, floor to ceiling, he gazed into the clouds as though he could find what he sought after there. His two-bed, modern styled, purpose built flat, overlooked Lewisham's biggest Tesco's car park. There was never a day it's been quiet. It was Lewisham, life of the party.

Often times he'd witness parents fussing with their children who either wanted to stay comfortably in the trolly or wanted to run around the car park, play 'tag' with their unwilling parent. Whenever he witnessed these interactions, he thought about his own childhood and what it was like, or would have been like if he tried one of those 'stunts' the children chose to pull. Death, or a trip to the hospital, depending on his father's mood, would have been on the cards for him. And this was not to say his dad was ever out with them to do big shops, or any at all.

Ricardo and David would be ordered to do the shopping with their mother. Their father, in earshot of her, would tell them to let him know if she was seen to be staring at any man for too long, or if she stopped to talk to another woman for too long. He would explain to his sons that their mother belonged to him and she was his property.

Property, that's how he was taught to view women. That's how he saw his mother, as property. She was owned. What she said had never mattered. Despite how tired she was after work, it was her duty, to cook. This had to be done within 30 minutes of setting foot in the house.

His dad, Grayson, was the head of the house. He would never let them forget it. He'd always repeat Ephesians 5 verses 22-23, 'wives submit yourselves unto your own husbands, as unto the Lord. For the husband is the head of the wife, even as Christ is the head of the church: and he is the saviour of the body.'

Ricardo's mind drifted into moments of hearing his father quote this scripture, and thought of how much of a mockery it was. He had never known his father to set foot in a church, but, for his transgressions, his narcissistic ways, he would quote the Bible.

The vibrant colours of Chick Corea's, Spain made an entrance into his thoughts with an urgency, startling him. Ricardo immediately returned to the present moment as his phone screamed for his attention.

"Yo G! Wah gwaan fam?" He spoke into the phone moving away from the window.

"What's good fam?" The voice on the other end responded. It was his friend Tony. Both have been friends for a majority of their 30 years of living.

Tony would often times laugh at Ricardo. He found it strange that Ricardo spent less time listening to legends like Tupac and Biggie. Or even, Kendrick Lamar. Ricardo's go to music was Jazz and Neo-soul, not Hip-Hop or Bashment. Their views, particularly those around Bashment, would lead to heated conversations, with Ricardo talking about his dislike for the degradation of women in some of the songs and Tony talking about looking beyond the lyrics and the 'good wine' to hold at parties and raves.

"What you on?" Tony's voice beamed through the phone.

"Don't even have a motive brudda."

"Say less. I'm coming through."

Ricardo chuckled. This was typical of Tony. He lived a care-free life, unfazed by anything thrown his way. His life was governed by impulse. The two were dissimilar, one sought validation, the other dismissed views and opinions held about him by others.

"What's going on with you and Shayla?" Tony asked raising the bottle to his lips.

Ricardo looked at his friend, brows scrunched up, shaking his head. He didn't believe there was anything with Shayla, she was simply there helping him to become a better version of himself.

"Nah, you can't give me that look.' Tony remarked. 'Which bitch you ever hear 'bout sending morning texts saying Dear Black Man and sending shit bout-"

"Yo watch what you're calling her man-"

"Seet deh! Defensive over me calling her a bitch. You never used to have a problem calling a woman a bitch, but all of a sudden, you're this knight in shining armour?"

With a clenched jaw, Ricardo gripped the neck of his bottle tighter. The disrespect his friend was showing seemed uncharacteristic to him.

"Relax man. You know I don't think she's really a bitch. It's-"

"Why is it so easy to just call her out of her name though? Why are we always quick to call women everything but their names at the least?"

Tony would never understand what ticked his friend off, but he did ponder the question. For him, it was second nature to call a woman a bitch. It came as easily as calling a Black male friend a nigga. The Ricardo Tony knew, was one who would never hesitate to call a woman out of her name, but something was different now. He possessed the attitude of a 'better' man.

"Sorry fam, just one of them tings I never thought about still."

"It's calm. Took me time to get to where I'm at you know, with my thoughts and that, how I look at women, and what I call them."

"Tammy still on your head top?"

"More than you'll ever know."

Both men sat back in the warmth of the smoke engulfing the room. Ricardo's mind wandered, imagining a possible life with Shayla. Before now, he never thought about what their lips would feel like if they had ever connected, or about if the shape of her body would fit into his as he hugged her.

There was a line with Shayla he never wanted to cross. He didn't know if that had anything to do with when they met, or her knowing his ex. It didn't feel right to him. Whatever it was, he didn't mind. He appreciated the friendship with her. Everything she taught him, he valued. He couldn't afford to lose her and didn't want to tarnish their friendship.

Letters in Black

118 Elm Tree Road

Lewisham

England

SE13 5SQ

8th June 2022

Dear

~~To the women I called a 'bitch' in the past~~

Dear

To the women I've called out of their names.

I've had countless conversations with my male friends, telling them how much of a bitch you were, because I got my ego was bruised. The craziest part, I never took responsibility for anything. It was always easier for me to make it seem as though you were the villain and 100% at fault.

Deflection was always the cure.

As a youth, one with a lost sense of identity, I never considered how my words about you to another, could cause harm. I think I have to say, this goes out to Howsa, more than anyone else. There was a day you and I disagreed about me generalising and grouping all women together. I was running on 'little d' energy. My attitude towards you, the things I said about women, was all uncalled for, damaging. I'm honestly sorry.

It's taken me this long, 18 years, to realise that I was a piece of shit. After our disagreement, I was talking to Jalen and some of his friends about the debacle, and this is where it gets mad. You will hate me more for this, you've got all the right to. We were all talking, drinking, smoking, all of that. We were gone! Frass! Doesn't excuse what happened, I know. Sadly, this was the state I was in. I sat with these guys in halls, cussing about you. I took it upon myself to take away your right to voice your opinion. I allowed my ignorance and ego to get in the way each time I opened my mouth.

Then one of the guys said, "these bitches need to know their place. They need to respect when we tell them something, they shouldn't debate or question it, just do it." I sat there like an idiot, agreeing. Hearing words similar to what my dad and uncle would say to me when I was a kid had me really sit there and agree with these guys. I wasn't even a man as yet. I was still 19. Imagine.

Howsa, Empress, I'm sorry for everything. My big mouth got you raped. What I sat there listening to and agreeing with, I hadn't realised this guy was serious. I remember him saying we should teach you a lesson. I remember being like 'yeah man she need to learn'. I wish I could go back in time and change that moment. I didn't understand the seriousness of what he was saying, so, I didn't think much about it all. Even if I did comprehend, I don't think I would have had it in me to say anything because the fool I was just finished talking badly about you.

I'm slowly learning though.

I can't change the past, but I can learn from it to help me from making the same mistakes. I know there are women similar to you who never got justice because of a bunch of reasons, like, not wanting to get into trouble, not wanting to be seen as a snitch, or even fear of not being believed. The issue with this is that, these are life altering crimes, and if no-one speaks up, no one gets held accountable. If there is no accountability, the cycle just will never end. I've learnt this from experience. I've been at the receiving end and I've also been the asshole.

I can only hope that women begin to feel safe enough to stand up to their perpetrators and get the justice they deserve. To hold on for so long to such toxins will only do nothing but kill you.

A lot needs to be done to give you and others in your position comfort in knowing that your voices will be heard. Women are forced to stay silent because the system doesn't always work in their favour. I'm not trying to say this to gain your forgiveness, and I know I will never truly understand all of the issues, but I think I understand enough.

If I knew how to help, I would.

Letters in Black

I've spent years being a part of the problem, but with the man I'm becoming, the man I've become, I want to be a part of the solution.

Again Empress, I'm sorry for everything. I know it doesn't mean all that much, but please believe when I say, I wish I knew better.

Chapter 4: **PROTECT**

Thursday, 9 June

Dear Black Man,

I owe you an apology. There was a moment in
time I believed in 'we must protect our Black
women'.I believed that Black women were being
failed, especially by our Black Men. Grossly incorrect.

I know now what was wrong with the slogan.
There are Black men who were unprotected little
Black boys. Black men who needed to be loved
as Black boys. How unfair it is to expect protection
from Black men who still need to be healed from
their pasts. I'm so sorry Black man.   5:32am

With one swift motion, Ricardo dropped his phone on the vacant pillow to his left, right hand covering his face, left arm outstretched, exhaling away the text he had just read. Agony rose within as the message found a way to get lodged in his system. A groan poured out of him, pained.

It was 6:16am; Shayla sent the message at about 5:35am, that's roughly the time she sent them, every day or there about for the past week. There was something in this which felt different. He wondered what was on her mind prior to her texting him. It was still early so he couldn't imagine it would be anything too thought provoking. But her words were so loaded, each sentence a new bullet. Each sentence, its own conversation starter. Each sentence carried different histories.

He questioned whether he was ready to face the day. Wiggling his toes, telling them it would soon be time to face the cold of the wooden floorboards he had chosen instead of carpets. Unwillingly, he stretched both hands towards the ceiling, slowly opening his eyes to be met by the sun's beam pouring through the window he left exposed before heading to bed last night.

"Alexa, play Here Comes Trouble by Chronixx." Ricardo managed to say with a defined grogginess to his voice.

Today's a Chronixx kind of day he agreed to himself, trying to think of an outfit to wear. There were no meetings planned for him today, so, the option of no blazer was winning. Nevertheless, he could almost guarantee that someone would find a way to change that. They had three uniform suit colours at his bank, black, grey or navy blue. The tie options were red with white stripes and red with black stripes. He settled on his black suit, excluding the vest. He was in no mood to be fully suited and booted today.

He thought more about the day ahead, mumbling through his things to do list, punctuated with grumbles and cursing when there was a task he was dreading. He remained as motionless as he could manage. The sun's beam grew stronger forcing the darkness behind his lids away.

Opening his eyes, he yelled into the void.

Ricardo forced himself to do the basic things, brush his teeth, wash his face, and shower. This was to be the easiest part. It should have been, yet, it presented to be more challenging than he could have ever asked for. Giving it no thought, he continued to get ready, skipping breakfast in the process.

Standing in front of his full-length mirror in the hall, he gave himself a once over. He nodded. *Look like somebody son today*, he said to himself, allowing a smile to briefly appear. His eyes travelled up his reflection, landing on the purple durag he wore to bed. Had he not taken it off now, he was likely to forget when he got to work. He brushed the waves that had been curated; working with their direction, his movements were cautious and deliberate. Satisfied with his efforts, he looked at the brush in hand, one he bought when on an escape visit to Barbados. The trip served him well, allowed him to get some sunshine and the space he needed to clear his mind. He returned the brush to its current home on the top of the white two-shelf bookcase he bought from IKEA two years ago.

Throughout the day Ricardo observed how Black women were treated when they came into the bank. He'd then compared that treatment with that of Black men. There wasn't any obvious mistreatment present, which he believed to be the case as it was their duty to treat each client with respect.

When he was out in public, he tried to observe for any differences there also, but, there was still nothing. He assumed this was because he wasn't integrated into the lives of these individuals.

While on his journey toward home after work, he overheard some teenagers, no more than 16 years old, talking about a video one of them saw online. Ricardo also saw said video, so listened closely to what they were saying, turning down the volume of his music.

"She aint wrong you know." Boy one commented. "You lot need all the sorries you can get. Always making tings seem like man dem fault."

"But if you do something wrong, aren't you meant to say sorry though? So… if you're gonna, be moving mad, tell me sorry for your bull-"

She was interrupted by boy one, who, with excitement shouted out "wait is Kayla gonna start swearing? Auntie will kill you fam." He jeered. "How will she? Whatever man" Kayla kissed her teeth at him. "Anyways, I can't fully agree with that woman, just because she said women need the sorry more than men, making it seem like we're feeble and that." She finished with hand akimbo.

"What I don't get was the thing about how women should say thank you instead of sorry." This opinion was voiced by boy two. "A woman does something wrong, or says something left and she says thank you, instead of sorry?"

"Alie!" Boy one interjected.

"What's wrong with that? Thanks for showing me your true colours so I can cuss you init?" Kayla and her girlfriends giggled.

"Everything! If a woman does something wrong, Kayla you just said this, if you're on some bullshit, you should apologise and say sorry."

"Actually... I said, she was tryna make women seem more feeble." She added with the infamous neck roll Black women were famously for.

The conversation grew louder causing commuters to stir in their seats holding on to the remaining comfort they had, as discomfort slowly set in. The older Black folks turned to face the group, scowling at them, while the older White folks stiffened in their seats, keeping their heads straight. Mothers with babies and toddlers rolled their eyes, while the men didn't seem to care, none but a man in his mid-thirties. Tall Black brother with locs. This guy, in the eyes of Ricardo, looked as though he worked on staying connected with the ancestors, wore beads around his neck and on his wrists.

He listened closely to the interaction taking place. Teenagers being asked to think beyond the surface of what they were taught. Why was it that they couldn't agree that men deserved to be apologised to. This played on Ricardo's mind, bringing him back to that which perplexed him the most in the morning. Shayla's text.

The next question latching onto his mind was, why did Shayla's text affect him as much as it did? A twenty-minute walk from the bus stop to his house did nothing for him but push him further into himself.

As if by clockwork, the second he crossed the threshold into his home, he received an email he scheduled last year to be sent to himself.

He remembered being a child and getting home from school he would have to strip once he'd gotten into the house and head into the shower. His mother would always have a basket for him and his brother to put their clothes into, or for him, throw his clothes into.

Had he ever missed putting lotion on his body, his mother would tell him, 'self-care is lotioning your melanated body.' He couldn't figure out if it was the saying which stuck with him, or the memories of his mother lightly dragging her freshly painted nails across his skin to test his ashiness, which made this part of his ritual as imperative as it was.

After the day he had, he chose to skip the gym, once again, and dinner. He wanted to jump into bed, but, was curious to find out what it was he sent to himself last year.

mailer@herestoyou.co.uk

The following has time travelled to you from the past. This was composed 9th June 2021 This is brought to you from HeresToYou.co.uk

Man like!

Can you believe you sat down and wrote an email to yourself? The idiot I am reread an email from Chloe back in 2019, June 1st, the one she sent when the piece ah man died innit.

I saw bare draft messages too. Do you still have them clogging up your email? The one that got me was the reply about her domestic violence case, then the draft you wrote after.

I'm curious to know, did you ever talk to mum about why she stayed with the sperm donor? What's David like these days? He used to run to daddy with every little thing about mommy. He got her in so much problems. What's his relationship with mommy like these days? How's our relationship with her? Is David still a way with women? How's his relationship with Eva? Has it gotten any better? Is he still treating her bad? How is he with Avery? Well, that's if you know, are you two even talking. Last question, did you ever ask either of the parents about why they never confronted Glen, and why they continued to send you back to his yaad?

I hope things are kriss for you. I would have hoped that you've moved out of the Banking life and doing something which makes you happy even though real talk, the role you've got is big. You need more than that life.

Bless up yuhself.

While reading, Ricardo experienced as many emotions as there were seasons in a day in England. He chose to read the emails mentioned and was taken on the adventure of a life time. He took deep breaths before venturing into the dungeon of his emails, and was able to finally find it, the email that sat in his drafts comfortably waiting to reap havoc.

from: Chloe Bennett <chloeb@bennettsinterior.co.uk>
to: Ricardo Bennett <r.bennett@gmail.com>
date: 01 June 2019, 07:13
subject: Re: Re: Hey cuz

22:33
1 – guardian angels reminder to remain faithful and to believe that everything is possible so long as you work hard.
2 – be kinder to the people you love and cut out the nagging when it comes to things that aren't important.

I think I like these. I'll do a deeper search later and then meditate; the numbers, the synchronicities, they help me to remain focused and in tune.

Yes twin, Bennett's Interior. Thank you. Started interior design 11 years ago and been in business for myself for the past 5. It's been one of the biggest blessings during some of my darkest days. I couldn't have asked for more to be honest. Life has been filled with so many ups and downs. My downs though, they were the definition of hell.

I used to think I was one of those women who would never end up in a relationship where my man would lay his hands on me, but boy was I wrong. I was as wrong as... I don't even know. I was just wrong. My boyfriend of 7 years almost killed me. He's an architect, well, was. He was an architect when we were together. We met when a client wanted my then company to meet their architect firm, and, he just so happened to be the architect on the project. We were talking for about 2 months before we got together, about a month after we finished working on the project, I couldn't bring myself to dating him while we were working together. Everything was good. For the first 3 years or so. Everything was bless.

I then started my company. He was trapped in his job, he wanted to escape but was scared to leave. He wanted to have his own thing, but couldn't bring himself to doing for him what I was doing for myself.

As my company took off, he started changing. I was putting together a portfolio from I was working my previous job and I had people there supporting me with getting my start. I don't know if it was him changing or if it was just everything becoming more apparent. I couldn't leave him. I kept telling myself he was just going through a rough patch and we could work through it.

That rough patch lasted a damn long time and to this day, I have periods where regret washes over me while walking with depression. When I say, the absolute worst feeling EVER! Ricky, it was devastating. I became a shell of myself. This man would berate me, say things like, you aint worth nothing. You think this business is gonna go nowhere? I will make sure you don't get no more client. He would go on and on. Then, one day he stepped to me with the shit, I looked at this man, dead in his eyes and I was like 'fam, why are taking out your shit on me? You're moving like it's my fault you aint got the balls to leave your job.' Who told me to open my mouth? This man rocked my jaw. What? I stepped to him like I was a G and he rocked the shit out of my jaw.

From then, whenever he started, he would come and start jabbing my head with his fingers. At times I wished instead of gun fingers he would actually just get a gun and shoot me. When we got into deep arguments, he used to drag me around the house with my hair tightly wound around his hand. The music was always blasting so neighbours wouldn't hear me scream.

It was my company, having a building to escape to which helped me to survive because, I couldn't tell my clients that I wasn't able to take on projects. That made no sense at all. I needed clientele so I could make my money.

I can't tell you how much I appreciate my family. I didn't realise that I had gone quiet on them, but months passed, my siblings couldn't get through to me and my parents hadn't heard from me. Even posting on social media, I hadn't done that in time and I wasn't thinking anything of it. All I know is, they turned up to my place one day, the day after one of my fights with him. My face was battered. Had my sister not forced me to give her a key to the house, who knows what would have happened.

My sister grabbed my essentials, laptop, chargers, clothes, anything she figured I needed for work while my mum escorted me out. My brother and my dad on the other hand, they were swearing up and down, wanting to wait till he got back. I had no strength to say anything, just, comply and let life unfold. Had he been in the house that day he would have died.

My mother is something different, she left a note saying, we're done. I won't be coming back. Don't look for me.' And that was it. I'm not fully healed, but I'm working on it. I'm seeing this family councillor. I'm in a relationship and pregnant, and I've got so much going through my head so needed the support. She's been extremely helpful.

I'm gonna leave this here though. It's a lot. Sorry if it's too much.

Chloe.

from: Ricardo Bennett <r.bennett@gmail.com>
to: Chloe Bennett <chloeb@bennettsinterior.co.uk>
date: 01 June 2019, 12:47
subject: Re: Re: Re: Hey cuz

Twin,

Sorry you had to go through all of that. I wish there's more I could say, but, sorry to know you had to deal with that ordeal. It's good to know your family stood by you and could tell something was wrong.

I'm happy to hear your business has been doing well all these years. My cousin's been a pro for years so I'm not even surprised.

Congrats on the pregnancy. I pray you have a safe delivery and hope the counselling sessions are helpful.

Stay bless cuz.

Ricky.

Drafts

from: Ricardo Bennett <r.bennett@gmail.com>
to: Chloe Bennett <chloeb@bennettsinterior.co.uk>
subject: Re: Re: Re: Hey cuz

He sounds like a prick. I get that he didn't want you to do better than him, but to stay with you and treat you the way he did? Nah, man's a prick. Me personally, I'd never get with a woman who was doing better than me, we'd be imbalanced, and how can I be anything for her if she's already everything and earning more than me? But to put my hand on a woman? That's dead.

I used to see my dad lay hands on my mum fam. He was never doing that shit in secret. He made sure me and my brother knew what was going on. The way he used to rough up mommy wasn't a joke ting. I remember the first time I saw her put on makeup. I asked what she was doing, and, I didn't recognise it then, but there was pain in her eyes. The pain wasn't even hidden. I can see it now. She looked at me and said it was just a little cover up. Dad had cut her under her eye with his ring when he backhanded her.

She was always beautiful to me, but that day, with the 'cover up', I didn't recognise any part of her beauty. I felt so helpless, but rage consumed me. She was weak and I wanted to protect her. In the same breath, I wanted her to protect me from Glen, but she couldn't even protect herself from my dad.

Why she stayed with him is beyond me. I guess now I look back at it, she might have thought she was doing it for me and David, to save us, to protect us. Those days David used to piss me off because nuff times he's the reason she'd get beat up.

I didn't even mean to make this about me. I'm happy you made it out. I'm happy you're with someone who you feel safe with. I hope it stays that way for life. You deserve the best.

Big love.
Ricky.

Chapter 5: **UNSPOKEN**

"What's going on brother?" David sauntered in as Ricardo looked on in shock. In one hand, he held two bottles of Heineken, in the other, he held a bottle of Wray and Nephew.

"I don't have nothing to chase that with yuh nuh." Ricardo managed to voice, referring to the Wray and Nephew held in his brother's hand.

The two had not spoken since David's last visit just over three weeks ago. David's impromptu visit caught Ricardo by surprise as he was a stickler for calling first to confirm that Ricardo was home. These pre-visit calls also served as a warning of some sort, there was little wiggle room for Ricardo to ever say he couldn't take any guests. Even so, David previously asked if he was a guest or family, twisting his younger brother's arm to force him to cave.

Both, together in the kitchen, opened their beer, while absentmindedly staring at each other. They had never been in this position before. They've had their differences, sure, but they had never shouted at each other the way they did.

Ricardo thought about all he should have said to David during his last visit. He should have called him out about how dismissive he was when talking about Avery. It was his disregard for her which pained Ricardo the most. A small voice in his mind attempted to encourage him to take the presented opportunity to let his brother know what was on his mind. All of this sounded like a grand idea, but he feared what would happen if he followed through.

David on the other hand, was trying to think of a way to break the ice and say sorry. He knew he was out of line for what he previously said to his brother, it was a moment of weakness for him. Had it been a situation around one of his students, he would have written up a referral to social services to get involved on the grounds of the child's safety being put at imminent risk. As the Safeguarding Lead at his school, staff depend on him to protect, not harm or endanger the children in their care. However, he downplayed that of his own blood. What was it that caused him to detach from her needs? Why did he disregard her wellbeing?

Sitting at his dinner table with his wife and daughter, he kept a tight lip, fearing if he spoke, he would say the wrong thing. Eva picked up on his vibe and asked him if he was okay, to which he repeatedly said, yeah, just tired. Avery was seemingly more reserved that evening, as though she knew what he said. He wanted to apologise; he wanted his princess to know how important she was to him. He wished he didn't add something else to the list of things his wife would tell him he need-ed to forgive himself for. No matter how he treated Eva, she somehow seemed to ask that he'd forgive himself. He loved her, but could never understand why she stayed whenever he mistreated her. He reminded himself of his father, abusive, dismissive and emotionally absent.

"What's going on with you D?" Ricardo's voice peered into the si-lence, slowly and carefully, checking to see if the coast was clear.

David couldn't string two words together to convince himself that he knew what was going on with him, let alone to tell his little brother.

"I'm trying to figure it out myself" he said, honest but distant.

"How's that?"

"Don't know where to start. I'm trying to make sense of life."

"I can drink to that."

Both men laughed, and in sync, placed their bottles on their lips, tilted their heads back, and took a swig.

David went on to telling Ricardo about the memorial. Explained that he saw how rigid Avery was, even suggested to his wife that she took her home.

Ricardo listened in disbelief. Based on their previous conversation, he would never have expected that of his brother. Knowing his broth-er, he would have never thought David would suggest anything to his wife, but he would have believed if he said he *told* her to take Avery home.

David regurgitated his memory of the evening from who argued to whose child turned out to be the Spawn of Lucifer. Most shocking, was the news about their parents, their mother had finally began looking into getting a divorce. Chloe's parents were the day's saviours. David, with great animations, described the highlights. "Her mum put every-one on blast, she cussed out everyone for being accomplices to Glen."

David continued, but his voice trailed off before finishing with "I didn't realise you were one of his victims. While Auntie Anita was telling mum and dad how disgusted she was as they stood by as silent contributors always sending you back, I died inside." He was yet to apologise for his previous behaviour, but, the longer they spoke, the more difficult it got.

Chapter 6: **GOD WHY**

Ricardo rolled over in bed knowing he wouldn't need to face the world for any reason today. Having turned his alarms off before bed last night and closing his drapes, his body clock deceived him, forcing him out of the lie in he asked the day for.

His manager was more than happy to grant him the time off as it's been a while since he took any. With nothing planned, excitement eluded Ricardo, allowing nerves to live rent free in his body. Three years ago, his last big break, he worked himself up and wound up in a situation which almost cost him his job and his life. Ever since, he had difficulties to request this much time and with the restrictions imposed in lockdown, travel out of the country was not particularly easy. He owed it to the avid readers who created social media content, reviewing and recommending books, for getting him through, and helping him maintain his sanity.

§§§

"What are you looking for in those books?" She asked, observing as his eyes rested on her feet.

"Something to make me think," he responded raising his eyes to her. "Something that will force me to be a better man."

"Better for who?"

"What do you mean better for who?"

"Exactly what I said. Better for who? You better not be out there looking other gyal."

"So, you're a gyal now? Not my woman?"

"Whatever." She chortled. "I'm happy with you as you are. You're perfect."

He swallowed. Heart pounding, racing for safety, he felt as though it was being taken away with the cycle, the loop of notes whizzing through speakers as Flora by Ludovico Einaudi poured into the room. She, Tamara, thought he was perfect, unbeknown to her, he was far from it.

She witnessed the change in his demeanour. The rigidity of his body. The tension flowing from his hand onto her feet. Her feet, the sole protectors of her body, were firmly clasped by his hands. She'd not be able to run if he chose to attack her.

Her voice, now clamped in her throat, battling to be free, chocked her. And barely above a whisper, she asked, 'what's wrong'?

At that point she imagined the worst. Maybe he was a serial killer, the kind who would befriend and 'date' his victims before their fatal day came. She knew that his relationship with his mother wasn't the absolute greatest, maybe that was his fuel. Maybe, he wasn't completely honest when he said that his relationship with his mother was tumultuous, when he told her that he'd witnessed his mother being abused by his father. Maybe it was the other way around, and his mother was the one who was abusive, and as he didn't have the power over her, he found the power over other women who resembled his mother, and toyed with their emotions before killing them.

She felt her heart pouncing through her chest wanting for her to escape, but she couldn't move. She was frozen. With his hands clasping her feet, she forced to remain calm, but knew it was futile. She had already worked her way up in a panic. How could she be so stupid? It hit her in this moment that she didn't know the man before her. They had only known each other for a month, only gone on 3 dates, and by their fourth date, she was sleeping at his house and started having sex with him. Didn't even do any tests before, she was reckless with him. He wasn't opposed when she suggested that their fourth date be at his house, she'd be happy to cook, but, being indoors sounded good. She wanted to poke her nose around, see how he lived to help her formulate an idea of who he really was.

Fast forward a year later, here she was, in his house, still with no idea of who he really was. All she wanted to do was learn more about him, and learn she did. She learnt more about his body and the movement of his hips with hers, how their lips would lock and how it felt when her legs were wrapped around him as he would navigate in her. She didn't know him besides that, in nothing but a short space of time, she could become his next victim. At her funeral, if she was able to have one, her family and friends would walk up to her coffin and scoff, tell her that she should have listened, maybe then she'd still be breathing.

Ricardo could sense her panic, and slowly released her feet from his grip. "Shit, I'm sorry. I-" He looked over at her, now curled up in the corner of the sofa. Standing, he walked over to the window, "look, there's some things about me I haven't told you but that's because I'm scared of ruining a good thing. We have got a good thing, right?" He asked as he looked over at her. With no reply, he continued, "I get if you wanna just leave now, run and never look back. I know I'm being elusive; I just don't know how to be open as yet you know." He finished his rushed thoughts turning his back to her, resuming his gaze, looking into the nothingness awaiting him.

Tamara wanted to ask, she wanted to poke the bear a little, just to get more out of him, but she wasn't sure she wanted to know exactly what he was talking about. In her mind, he sounded like a killer. "How many people have you bodied?" Her voice quiet, cautious, asked Ricardo.

With confusion dancing on his face, he turned to look at her once again. "Wait, you think I've killed people? Is this why you-?" His voice trailed off before an explosive wave of laughter flowed through his body.

"Babe-", his head thrown back, "you thought, me-", struggling to laugh and speak. "You thought, man like me, I bodied people?"

Tamara looked at him, this man before her, literally laughing his head off, unsure if this was a ploy. Was he a psychopath? Sociopath?

Ricardo, recognising that she was indeed being honest, forced his laughter to fade. How he managed to obscure her view of him was something he needed to understand. He couldn't allow her to continue to believe that this was his truth.

§§§

As Ricardo laid back in bed, he started thinking about what life would have been like had he not experienced some of the things that were thrusted upon him. It would take a lot for him to come to terms with the cruelty he faced.

Reviewing his childhood, he was unable to decipher if some of the scenarios were fantasy or reality. Could this have been the reason his parents had never stepped in? Could he and Chloe have imagined some of the things they went through as children? Was it possible they imagined the same experiences? Could this have been the reason parents took no notice and didn't act on it? Had he and Chloe only witnessed the things their uncle was guilty of and allowed their overactive imagination to take the lead? Could that be a thing? Were his relationships ruined due to fallacies? Was that at all possible?

Tears rolled down his cheeks as thoughts raced through his mind. He wanted to forgive himself, but didn't know where to start. A steady stream of tears poured out of him as he questioned his purpose in life. *Why me?* Roared from his mouth repeatedly. He knew that there was some truth, if not all, based on his experiences. He knew that he was molested as a child. He knew his uncle was the perpetrator. He knew he was encouraged to touch Chloe inappropriately. But, he didn't know if his uncle was sick enough to teach him how to penetrate her. To rape her. There were parts of his childhood he blocked and as much as he would like to know the truth, he didn't know what he would do with that truth.

There was a level of honesty, a wall he built, stopping him from sharing all with anyone about this ordeal. He had never sat with his parents to be open about his experiences as a child. The most he told them, while they kept sending him back to his uncle's house was that, he didn't like to go to uncle Glen's house. He didn't know how to be honest with them. Glen had also brainwashed him into believing that his parents would scold him for saying such a thing.

He wanted to forgive the little boy in him for not being more outspoken about his experiences. He wanted an apology from his family, but he needed to apologise to himself first. His tongue cursed God for allowing him to live in the abuse. He argued with God for allowing children to fall victim to molesters. How could a God so mighty not stop men from harming the innocent? How wrong it then becomes when people accuse the innocent turned guilty for what they do. He was innocent. He had no control over his actions after what his uncle did. He wasn't deeply religious, but he knew God was out there controlling this world he lived in. Maybe in another universe there was a different entity in control, but within this realm, he knew God had the ultimate power, so couldn't understand why a God so powerful wasn't taking charge of the cruelty faced by the innocent children He allowed to enter this world.

He picked up his phone to send Shayla a reply, albeit late, but still a reply to let her to know that he now understood what she meant about men needing to be protected. It all made sense to him. Left with his thoughts, not needing to worry about what suit he wanted to wear today, or how on point his waves were before leaving the house. His thoughts held him captive.

Having been so caught up in the web he wove for himself, he saw a text that came through from Shayla, her usual Dear Black Man message. *I wonder if I'm the only one she sends these to.* He stared at the screen in his palm, as his new found friend, thoughts, continued to surge through his mind. What would his life had been like without her, had he not spoken to her that night? They never dated, he was never interested in her like that. They were close, he could tell her whatever was on his mind without the fear of being judged. She was understanding and willing to call him out on his bullshit. He needed a woman like her in his life but didn't want to allow himself to have feelings for her. She taught him more about himself than anyone had ever done across his life. None of his friends would allow him to spend time introspecting to develop himself as a main character in this life, or any life as a matter of fact. Not his friends, nor ex-girlfriends.

He raised his eyes from his phone looking above as though he could see God and His angels laughing at him. Shayla's text wasn't confirmation of sorts, but aligned with his thoughts. He wanted to reply with 'who sent you', but when you know better and know God shows up through people, you know who sends the messages you need.

Unintentionally the tears that were on pause resumed once more as he read Shayla's message:

Dear Black Man

What are your biggest fears? Did they come up because of past traumas? Did you talk yourself into believing these things could ruin you? What's the reason behind those fears? Can I help you to overcome any of them?

Love you Black Man.

Had she been aware that her message would send him into overdrive, maybe she would have kept it sitting in her drafts. Maybe she would have skipped today's text. But she wouldn't have known. She would not have been aware that this would cause him to break down more than he had done before.

She had no clue what Ricardo was going through and she wouldn't have any idea, not before the day ended because this was a struggle of his. He was unable to be as vulnerable as he wished to be; there was no blueprint for him to follow. He learned best from examples laid out as a clear path for him to know what the expectations were. His academic successes were testament to the benefits of examples for him. He remembered approaches in exams and had never failed. He saw reality as the same, but while there was none in previous life, he couldn't tell what his next steps were to be.

What are your biggest fears? The question moved into his thoughts, with all of its baggage, everything it hoarded over the years, crying out for his attention. *What was it? What were they? Am I afraid of turning out like Glen? Spending the rest of my years behind bars? Am I afraid that the truth held within would consume and eat away at my flesh until I became non-existent? Could it be that my truth would escape and those closest to me, Shayla, would shun me? He wanted to know the answer but he was afraid to find out.* He knew an answer required him to respond to it in order to become a better version of himself.

One of his fears was being a parent who valued screen time more than family time. He saw enough of it around, being in coffee shops observing families as they would come in, two children, mum and dad, both children being owners of tablets, engrossed in a kid's programme and both parents on their phones either checking emails, or messages of some sort, or swiping away at some form of social media drug. The interaction with their children was minimal, the younger of the two was attended to when being forced to sit in a particular position so he could eat.

What Ricardo found funny in this situation was the struggle the parents faced when trying to peel their children away from the screens. The negotiation that took place was second to none. Mum took a toilet break leaving dad to get the children together. He attempted to put his feet down to show he was in charge of these little bodies which housed souls bigger than life itself. Though this was comedic to Ricardo, he couldn't face becoming a parent.

The sun crept in through a gap in his drapes, attempting to flood the room with brightness, reminding Ricardo that it had broken bread with the sky. He let out a low groan, nose stuffy, eyes closed, he placed the heel of both hands atop his head, dragging them down across his face. He reminded himself that he did not need to do anything today. To exist, to inhale and exhale, to simply be, was enough of a win. He didn't need to do anything, thus, he switched his phone off, pulled the covers over his head, rolled over and nodded off.

Chapter 7: **LOVE**

118 Elm Tree Road
Lewisham
England
SE13 5SQ
14-Jun-2022

To my mother,

I love you. I truly do, or at least, I believe I do. Sometimes I try to think about what love means and how it can be shown or received and it makes it difficult for me to decide whether I do love you. Is it normal for someone to question if they love their parent? Shouldn't this be a natural thing? Shouldn't it be normal?

Mum, why was I never encouraged to be open about my feelings? Why was I never given the opportunity to grow up in a safe environment? What kept you living with my father for so long? Was it because of David and me? Is that the case? Is that it? Is that why you wouldn't spend time with us as we got older? Is this why you were happy to dump me on Glen? Even after auntie Anita stopped sending Chloe. Even after I said I didn't like going there.

Why was it only me who you would take to Glen's? Why was David never over there? What was it about him that made him get special treatment? I know I'm a grown man, but I need answers. Is it possible that you wanted me to spend time with Glen because he was my father? Is that it?

I wish I was able to come to you and tell you what was going on when I was with Glen; the things he made me to do Chloe, the things he did to me, the things his girlfriend did to me. This man mocked me, laughed at me, made me a prisoner of his twisted mind.

I saw how he would manipulate his girlfriend. I saw how he controlled Chloe, through me. All of that. His words stuck with me, and you know who ended up on the receiving end of all of that? Niyah, when we were kids. Avery, some years ago. You remember the big fiasco? I got drunk that night, was at David's babysitting, but instead of being a decent adult, I was touching up my niece? I was a big man at that time, so honestly had little excuse, but some of that blame is to be placed on Glen. On you. On dad. By you both not listening to me, not allowing me to speak up, you enabled Glen to continue to do the shit he was doing to me. It stayed with me, for years.

No word of a lie, there were days I wanted to end my life because I couldn't live with myself knowing what I went through. These were situations no one would talk about and look, I turned out to be nasty, just like Glen. Tell me he's my dad. Tell me the apple doesn't fall far from the tree. It's things like this mum, things like this really make me question if I love you.

All of the fights I got in when I was in school, I didn't know how to control my anger. A lot of that anger didn't even have anything to do with the guys I got into fights with. Most of it stemmed from being forced to bottle up years of pain. There was so much I held on to before exploding. Being excluded helped me a lot. It gave me time to lock away in my room and just be one with me. You'd be at work, dad would be at work or out of the house, somewhere, and, David would be at school. This was always best for me. I didn't have to talk to anyone, I didn't have to pretend to be okay. I used those days to cry. I would spend hours in the shower. Remember when the water bill would come up high? I guarantee, if you were to get my school record and check those bills, they were always highest when I was at home.

Sometimes, I instigated fights just because things were too much for me and I would have flashbacks of my childhood. I didn't know how to say I needed a day out for my mental health. Hell, I'm still learning how to say this. Thankfully I've gotten over the past years, if not, I know I'd never be able to keep a job. I'd be in and out of prison, like that cousin of mine no-one ever wants to talk about because he let the family down. Has anyone ever stopped to think that maybe the family let him down?

Has anyone in the family ever taken accountability as a measure to say maybe all he needed was some guidance? Maybe he needed love. We all know he lacked love. He lacked a stable home, but everyone acted as though he was okay. He was never taken on family trips; he was never included, so was it ever a surprise that he would find a family outside of the family? Our family is a joke. We don't know what it means to be a family.

We just have people we share blood with but no one to look out for us. We were never a village. Children were never put first.

You were never my village. You never put me first. How can I love the woman who brought me into this world but taught me nothing about love? I want to be able to find peace in our relationship. I want to look past the disdain I felt towards you as a child. I know my childhood was shit for you. You lived with a man who put you through hell, so I want to see past that and rebuild the bridge that was broken between us. I want you to want the same for us to both get to that point.

I hope one day we can get there. In the meantime, I'll hold on to hope. Hope seems to be more committed than you ever were.

This is to the future I hope we can have.

Ricky.

Letters in Black

118 Elm Tree Road
Lewisham
England
SE13 5SQ
14-Jun-2022

To my father,

What happened? You couldn't have always been the asshole you were who abused his wife. What switched got flipped for you to treat her the way you did? Tell me you loved her at one point in your life. There were so many pictures of you both smiling, that was before I became a known factor in the world. What was it that changed? Was it something to do with me? I personally believe this was the case.

What happened? I've seen how you treated other women; you actually treated them like Queens, but mum? I'm sure not one soul would believe her if she were to tell them that you used to drag her around the house like a rag doll. If my mother was meant to be honest with your family, they wouldn't believe her. I don't think they really like her much either so you'd have definitely won that.

You know what else? There's a trophy with your name on it. That one's for teaching me and David how to treat women like shit. You know he demeans his wife in public right? He talks down to her, calls her stupid, if anyone compliments her, he scoffs or laughs. I've seen him reduce her to tears. I'm sure underneath it all he claims that he loves her. I think he may now be working on treating her better, but over the past years? Yeah, he put her through hell. Not forgetting his daughter. Thought my brother would have filed charges against me, he didn't. What he wanted though was for me to be in the same room as his daughter, not alone, but it's still just as bad. His daughter who I harmed, the daughter I messed up, he invited me to be in the same space as her and when I told him I couldn't do that to her, her wellbeing went out of the window. This guy told me that she wouldn't remember anything because of how long ago it happened.

And as for me? It's a big thing with me. Not only did you play a part in the destruction of your second child. You assisted Glen in turning me into the monster I became. That started when I was young. Disgusting fam! You remember Chloe? Anita and Clive's daughter? Yeah, remember when we used to go to Glen's yard? Glen used to make me touch her up. But you knew that already, didn't you? You found out from your sister, the bullshit that was happening at Glen's yard, but did you even care? It wasn't a lie. Your brother, would force me, your son, to touch up your niece. I can't remember if he made me penetrate her. And I can't tell you to ask him because he's dead and gone now. Rotten out. I don't even want to know, but I wouldn't be surprised if that shit happened. Before everything transpired, Chloe and I were close. Back then the devil danced in the eyes of Glen and invited himself to what should have been family time. Hell was closer to us than we could have ever imagined. That's the role you played in the Glen debacle.

Now that's just Chloe. How about Niyah? You must remember her. Your wife didn't like her. Now I think about it the whole family was a mess! Your side. Mum's side. Jah know, couldn't have ask for a better family to land in, right? But Niyah! You made me believe that the only way to get a female to do things my way was to manipulate her. Glen taught me to be sexual. You taught me to be physical and psychological. What a mix!

It gets better. I have NEVER been able to hold down a relationship. The way I saw you beat and harass my mother, I never wanted to be like you so if a woman got me mad to the point I thought I would hit her, I had to walk. It's jokes, I never wanted to hit a woman, but as a kid I was okay with sexually assaulting others. What a madness?

Well done though. Father of the year.

I just want to know what happened. Other than Glen, the rest of your siblings are actually calm. Anita protected her daughter. She found out about what Glen was doing and removed her daughter from the situation. You guys were told and clearly, I didn't need the protection. You kept sending me back. You did say once that I needed to be around Glen, didn't you? I couldn't have dreamt that could I? Am I going to one day find out that this man was my father? Is that why you beat mum the way you did? Is this why you favoured David over me?

Letters in Black

I wish I had a better childhood. It was difficult for me and I'm not proud of the person I became. I deserved to be loved as a child. I needed to be taught how to channel my emotions. I needed to know that I was valued. I needed to be taught what love looked like. It would have saved me from the work I'm doing now to get my life in order. I, too often, feel damaged. I wish I knew better then, but wishing won't help anything right now, so, I might as well just pray for healing. Prayer would work better than a wish, wouldn't it?

I'm done though.

Ricky.

Chapter 8: **FIGHT**

Wednesday, 15 June

Dear Black Man,

I can't stop thinking about how much I've been censoring this in my mind. I've been wanting to send this for a while now, but could never think of the right time. I don't even think there is ever a right time to mention this, but I hope this isn't a bad time. As you keep reading you'll see why I've waited till the now to text you.

I'm sorry you were molested as a child. I'm sorry you've had to be so quiet over the past number of years. Being a man was taught to you in the worst way. You were taught that no matter what happened, being a man meant you were to remain silent. I'm sorry you are one of the unknown victims.

I'm sorry that you've had no-one in your corner. I'm going to be her, the woman who makes noise on behalf of men who were sexually abused, as children, as teenagers, even as adults. It's not fair that we only hear about the 'choir boys' who were touched and assaulted by priests, but never about the little Black boys molested by family and family friends.

Please understand, you have an ally in me. I'm here to make all the noise for you and make this a known thing until you are able to join me in this fight for justice.

Love you Black Man.   5:32am

Thank you, Queen. Thank you for being you and
thank you for this message. I can't tell you how
much it means to me. I don't know if I will ever be
able to get over it, but I want to get through it. I
want to become better for me, better for my friends,
better for my future Mrs, better for my children. I
can't see myself moving forward until I get through
this fire. Thanks for supporting me. Thanks for not
mocking me. It means the world to know I have
5:45am   someone who genuinely cares.

I'm happy to be here for you. You're doing a
great job. I know it's not always easy, but you're
doing really well and I don't ever want you to
lose hope King. Your efforts will not be in vain
and your future will reward you greatly.   5:49am

Ricardo tapped the call icon after letting go off the air he so desper-
ately clung to. He couldn't bring himself to continuing the conversation via text. Everything in him was crying out to get into the depths
of it all, say what was on his mind without deleting a chunk of his
thoughts, and today felt right to speak Shayla. Tell her about some of
the things that has been on his mind, if he could find the courage to
pull the cat from his tongue and free his words.

He counted the 'brrrings', as he liked to call them, trying to think
of a conversation starter if Shayla did answer. As it got to the fourth,
he hesitantly hovered his thumb over the red icon, still hoping she'd
answer but half hoping that she didn't. It has been some time since he
has spoken to his friend on the phone and there were days, he couldn't
bring himself to responding to her messages, which caused him to be
filled with extreme anxieties.

"Hey!" Her perky voice came through his phone.

Here goes, Ricardo gathered himself. "How you doing? Hope I
didn't disturb you."

"Don't make me laugh. Disturb me from what? Have you seen the
time?"

"You could have been exercising, doing yoga, sleeping-"

"Can you see me rolling my eyes?" She chuckled.

Ricardo laughed at his friend's response. *Maybe the conversation will be okay,* he thought, though they've only been talking for one minute fourteen seconds... Fifteen... Sixteen... Seventeen... Eighteen... Nineteen... His eyes locked on the time as he listened to the comfort she brought. It felt good to hear her voice, to feel her laughter fill both her room and his. Somehow, Shayla was always the person who allowed her being to completely take up the space around her.

Shayla was the blessing he had no idea he needed. He was never aware of the void within him, or his subconscious biases and views toward women before beginning to spend time with her. Could he have imagined that the orange line connecting East London to South transported blessings such as Shayla? If he believed in the definitions of colours, what they meant, what they depicted, he would be able to raise his hands and say, *yeah, I knew it was coming, just didn't know my gift of life would be in the form of a Black Woman.*

Their conversation veered through the 'how are yous' and 'what's news with yous', meandering along the infamous trenches of 'so what have I missed' catch up, all the while teetering on the edge of the text.'

Shayla always presented as confident and level-headed. Ricardo was always unable to recall a time he saw her flustered or heard her question her abilities. For instance, a barbecue last summer, Ricardo being Shayla's self-appointed hype man, pointed out to a group of friends that she was at the top of the class when it came to not being verbally destructive towards one's self. He listened in on the silence that grew between them trying to figure out what was potentially going through her mind. He wondered if she was thinking about how she would approach the conversation they both knew was around the corner.

"Thanks-" a soft voice escaped him.

"What for?"

"Had it not been for you, I would have stopped trusting people all together."

Shayla remained quiet, processing what he said, but also giving him the opportunity to free more of himself in the space created. This was unexpected to say the least, but she trusted that he needed this moment.

After treating him to dinner in January, they went for a stroll over Waterloo Bridge taking them from Spaghetti House in Holborn, to Waterloo Station. Their conversation took turns between laughter and withheld tears. Anger raged within the walls of her body as Ricardo shared the ghosts of his childhood. Shayla learned quickly that there were times all he needed was for her to listen. With time, she became an expert in listening to him.

Ricardo finally understood what it meant to be loved and seen. He knew Shayla was a blessing, and had saved him from himself. She saved hell from having to put up with him, who he was. She knew what he had to offer to the land of the living, but he was oblivious. He was blind to the knowledge held in love, in being within someone's vision, their line of sight.

As the word *thanks* snuck out from his mind through the partition of his lips, awakening his vocal cords, he saw the meaning of love begin to wash over the painting of his childhood and the lack of what he needed. His breathing marinated in anxieties flittered, wanting to regain confidence to continue with his speech.

Ricardo and Shayla embraced the atmosphere around them, neither one rushing to say anything before the other. Shayla read the silence to herself as it handed her a list of reasons why she should remain patient. Ricardo wanted to wish this moment was one he was spending alone with a pen in hand and sheets of paper being caressed by of his left hand with his right hand pulling that which had been written on. With it not being the case, knowing he opened a portal he'd not be able to close, he drew in a breath to coat the lining of his lungs before continuing.

"You came into my life at a time when I was dying. I can't even tell you how close I was to letting go off hope; I was losing the will to face each day. I felt like I was standing on the edge of the cliff waiting for the moment something would push me over. I had no reason to stay."

He paused, contemplating whether being transparent with Shayla was the right way to go about things. If he prayed, would God grant him his request? Allowing this moment to loiter without being reminded of this instant, the one he chose to be honest, he wondered if this was the right way to go about it. Was Shayla the right person to expose himself to?

You do not grow up with a mother who reminded you that whatever happened in the house was to be swept under carpets, to become an adult who feels comfortable to share all that feels wrong with him. This was a conversation he was never able to share with his family, he'd already thrown the thought of doing so out of his mind. There was no level of warmth which would make him feel safe in doing so. And to now have someone who was always ready to be by his side as he rode the waves of this journey, he was to call life, was scary.

"When we met, I was spiralling out of control. I started drinking more, had the falling out with David, and guilt became the demon who paid me visits each waking moment. I needed to find a way to silence it all. I didn't want to continue living."

The wound of his anxiety now reached beyond where it begun. It left a gaping hole in his throat as his words morphed into soft sobs. Ricardo offered himself the opportunity to let the tears cleanse him, apprehension had no room to weld up within. There was little time to think about what would be next. A small part of him wanted to stop the tears from finding security in rolling down his cheeks. That small part of him didn't want his body to produce more tears and snot. The ugly. He didn't want her to hear him ugly crying. Having been mocked by his boys in the past, this small part of him was scared that Shayla would also do the same at a later date, something he didn't need to be reminded of.

"I-" he stopped. As his honesty now developed, it was apparent to him it was taking on the form of reality before him.

"Would you believe if I told you that I took time to plot my escape from the world? I looked into male suicide rates, expecting that I would have handed over my body to the statistics. You know it was back in the

60s when women gave power to their voices, their suicide rates went down? But men? Ours went up. Mad init?"

Shayla knew it wasn't a statement, nor a question which required a response. Her heart was steadily picking up pace. She wasn't angry at him for wanting to remove himself from life's equation. She instead was angry at the caregivers of his inner child. Those who were meant to share love with him. Those who were to teach him that he was valuable. She too battled with depression and knew what it felt like as it crawled over her skin like a curse mark bestowed to be activated whenever she was feeling too good about life. It was a small, yet painful reminder that maybe she wasn't to settle in being comfortable.

She wished she could express to him that he too saved her. Meeting him, having room to be honest, as best as she could, would give her a change of heart towards herself. She would forgive herself for not being a better friend to who she was. She would forgive herself for not trusting her parents. She met a man who had a heart that was made to be shared and appreciated, it saved her.

"I-" Ricardo's words revved up again. "I've not been a hundred percent with you. I kinda told you about Avery, but I wasn't fully you know, truthful about what happened. I wanted to tell you the other day when I told you about my uncle and what he did to me and Chloe. I've been shook to tell you because I don't wanna lose you."

The silence reclaimed its identity in their conversation, this time forcing to refrain from spewing hate. It grew into one of the monsters he knew a little too well. Shayla could only guess what it is he meant, but feared intruding on his thoughts, scared to push him into a position which would cause him to retreat into the shell he broke out of.

"David asked me to stay in with Avery one evening because he wanted to do a ting for his wife. They were going through a rough time but these times I was dealing with a lot. Broke up with my girl because she didn't think I was open enough with her. She was right. I was hiding tings from her. The way I felt. Things I had been through. Just me. I was hiding who I was. So, yeah, we broke up and I started seeing a therapist because real talk, I wanted to be better for her. I used to do a lot of reading to try better myself but she said she was happy with me as I was and I got complacent in all of that, so I stopped.

I lied to her you know, we were chatting and it was bad enough she thought I had killed people, so I had to come out with a quick lie because I thought that was the best way forward. It was after that she was like nah, we're done because you're hiding shit and don't know how to be honest. Now, after all of that, my mental declined. Everything my uncle used to say about how to make sure a woman is doing things the way you want, started flooding back. These times I was blazing on a regular and drinking hard. Got to David's yard with liquor in my system, and when him and Eva left, I kept drinking. I wish David smelled the liquor and weed on me. I wish he knew me better because he would have hopefully told me to go home and find other arrangements for Avery. Now, because that didn't happen, I was there and Avery was meant to go to her bed but decided that she wasn't gonna listen to me this time round, so, I was like, aight, little girl want to act like big woman, let me show her what happen to big woman at night."

Like blood after the knife has been removed from a wound, the words, his past, gushed out full force. Shayla embarked on a journey toward understanding how complicated this man she had cultivated a relationship with was. She wanted to hate him, hang up and never speak to him again. She wanted to cut him off completely, but there was a nagging feeling holding her hostage on the phone.

To understand him was what he needed most. There was no doubt about that. He never had anyone to share this with and though he now had Chloe, he couldn't imagine that he would have the strength to be vulnerable with her about the pain and mistrust he, as an uncle inflicted upon his niece.

"I'm sorry," he feebly uttered.

"There's nothing to be sorry about."

"But there is. I just dumped everything onto you without even asking about your capacity."

"I'm your support system."

"And support systems don't deserve to have problems dumped and emptied on them just like that."

Shayla couldn't dispute it. She's always been told she is too kind and needed to set boundaries, but something about Ricardo's story compelled her to give him the room to release. She's always known how little support there is out there for men, having been raised by a single father. The man who raised her, fought for her, she witnessed firsthand, the struggle he faced. Society rarely offered him a hand in being all he could for her and her siblings. And this bothered her deeply. So to receive emails from big supermarket brands asking if individuals wanted to opt out of Father's Day emails, crushed her spirit enormously.

It angered her that men such as Ricardo were demonised without being understood and she knew she had her biases that would have stopped her from caring about anything further he would have to say. Without knowing his past, she would have lost interest in the conversation before he would have been able to share his truth. She would have made an assumption as he, with complications, skirted around the main part of this conversation.

Society, communities, didn't create safe haven for men to seek the help they needed. Advocates were needed for men, especially Black men who have always been demonised. A bad taste has been left in the mouths of all, particularly Black women, due to slavery. The conditioning over hundreds of years to believe that Black men are villains, is one of the most detrimental positions to be in. She couldn't condone what Ricardo did, and nothing about what he said gave the impression that he was seeking a thumbs up for his mistakes, but he needed to let it all out. He was never heard and when he was seen, it was a result of him matching a description or having been wrongly accused, used as a scapegoat. As a Black man, he would always been deemed as a monster yet no-one knew the stories, he held captive. She wanted him to feel comfortable sharing these stories with her as she recognised this was something he needed.

"I don't know what to actually say Ricky-" Shayla opened up. "I can't condone what you did to your niece, but I hear you. I hope you don't go pinning all of this on anyone. Not on your uncle or your ex, or on your therapist. They can't get the brunt of the blame, you will need to take some responsibility, a lot of it at that. I'm not saying you aren't already doing so, but I just need you to understand how I feel about this. You've taken the time to be vulnerable with me, and I can't not share how and where I stand with all of this."

"Yeah."

Their motif found this to be the right time for a reappearance, seeking permission to exist amongst them with Ricardo's cries returning to a state of soft tears. The permission to loiter was rejected by the scarcity of time. As much as Shayla would have loved to remain on the phone with him, she was unable to. Adulthood required her to work.

She left Ricardo with love, blessings, and a prayer that he would be able to truly forgive himself, his family, and his life, in hopes to allow him to find a greater peace.

The rest of his morning was spent with prayers being raised asking God for guidance. Shouts, asking God why He allowed such evil to exist on Earth. And praises, thanking Him for blessings bestowed upon him in the form of people such as Shayla.

He no longer wanted to believe in the saying, misery loves company, a path he was given to follow. More was needed to be able to survive the life in which he was to participate in.

How he had such an understanding friend, one who would teach him and hold him accountable, was beside him. He was grateful for everything Shayla presented to him. Without her, his life would have kept its bleak outlook, and that's to say he hadn't gone through with attempts to leave permanently.

Shayla knew that society rarely gave scope for Black men to represent their truths, and to now find out from a man she knew personally that what he faced was hardly ever spoken about, lit a fire in her. Ricardo, though he has previously been honest with her, still had never before disclosed this much information to Shayla, and she wasn't mad about it.

Ricardo felt relieved to share with someone who would not laugh at him, like the interviews he'd watched where Black men would talk about the abuse they went through and it was dismissed with them being laughed at by the interviewer. It's as though the phenomenon is a comedy script. It's not taken seriously and it makes sense as to why more men don't step forward. He was angered knowing that there were men in his position who would be unable to open up to anyone, friends or strangers, seeing that their pain was met with laughter.

Light is rarely shed on the men who have been molested as children, as teenagers, as adults. They feared being called gay if they said that they have been molested or raped by a man. Because no matter how progressive we say society is, being a homosexual is still, in the eyes of some, frowned upon heavily. The thought processes passing through minds, didn't add up. Instead of believing that this isn't only a possibility, but actual reality. There were folks who put it down to men lying about being straight, saying they're on the downlow.

Men also can't say they have been raped by a woman, because the Sexual Offenders Act in the UK states that a woman can't rape anyone because she doesn't have a penis. Women would then get away with their crimes for the simple reason, men, knowing a woman would not be charged with rape, would not report it. And dare he be honest to say to friends, or family, this was the case, he would be ridiculed by them. He would be laughed at as they ask 'how does a man allow a woman to sexually assault him?'

How can a man feel comfortable, confident enough, to step forward and pick out his offender, if his offender is a woman? How can he feel brave enough to call out the man who invaded his personal space and stole his sense of being? Violating him?

Not only was this bothersome for Ricardo, the matter also infuriated Shayla. It meant everything to her that her friend regained his identity, found himself as a man, that he would be able to step up in life and prove to himself that he was more than the past that was never confronted by his parents. She wanted to bring it up, but didn't know how to. She didn't know if he would be ready to have this conversation on the phone with her.

118 Elm Tree Road
Lewisham
England
SE13 5SQ
15-Jun-2022

Dear Avery,

First, I must ask you to forgive me for my wrong doings. No matter what I say, I can't pretend that I was never in the wrong. I hurt you in a way I know has caused you years of pain, and healing only comes in short, careful bursts.

I never meant to hurt you. I know that's easy to say and it doesn't make anything better, but please understand. I had not planned to do to you what I did. Alcohol is one hell of a drug and having been so far under the influence of it, in the mental space I was in, I acted out of character.

You didn't deserve that and I can only ask that you believe me when I say, I wish it never happened.

I don't know how many sleepless nights you've had. Or how many dreams of yours have been haunted. What I do know is that you've become another number, which I hope does not get added to the suicide list.

You were such a smart girl growing up, I may have interrupted this, but I want for you to know that what I did to you should never cause you to change the definition of who you are. Again, I know it's easy for me to say, but it's a lesson I've learned in recent times. I held on to anger for so long not realising that I lost my identity, though to be frank, I had never known myself. When I was old enough to form an identity for myself, it was stolen.

Letters in Black

I was younger than you were, please understand this is not me asking for your sympathy, or your empathy, it's just an explanation of how and when I lost my identity. I was younger than you were, would be sent to Uncle Glen's along with my cousin Chloe, and it was all good at first. We used to get left with him when our parents went out. Now, after a while, going to Glen's, he used to put on dancehall and said he was teaching us how to have a good time. He wanted us to learn like kids in Jamaica. Apparently, they would have days where there would be big speakers put up in the playground at school, kids were allowed to wear whatever they wanted, and they even had funfair and food.

That description made Chloe and me wish we were living in Jamaica. Big music. Big energy. Big vibes. We wanted to enjoy that life so we were eager to learn how to dance. What a start right? He had us hooked. We knew we had cousins in Jamaica, we wanted to be like them. We were caught. That's where it all started. Teach us how to dance. Not only were we learning to do these dances, we were each other's dance partner.

As kids, we knew to some degree that we shouldn't have been up on each other the way we were, but it was our uncle who we trusted. Our parents trusted him with us, we had no real reason to be weary of him.

Everything's blurred now. I have tried my hardest to repress the memories because they have been nothing but torture to me for years. This is why I know that what I did to you won't be easy for you to forget. Dissociation is great, but when these things aren't targeted, when there is no method for healing implemented, it all floats back to the surface, forms an iceberg, you become the Titanic, not knowing how to navigate around it, and when you crash, survival strategies may not activate. I want you to get therapy. I need your parents to find you a therapist. You need this to survive. You need this to be the best version of you.

I started therapy at one point but my therapist wasn't right for me. A white man who couldn't envision what things were like for me, a Black man. He couldn't understand that the house I came from wanted me to be a hardened individual and I was never taught how to trust. I could have tried to find a therapist who would understand me, but I didn't want to be judged by a Black man or Black woman, so I never rescheduled with anyone else.

For years I struggled with knowing who I was. I felt so dirty for everything that happened with Chloe. I blamed myself for being compliant. I couldn't forgive myself. I tried to talk to my parents, but they didn't really want to hear it. I felt like a demon. There were nights I couldn't sleep, and when I did, the memories flooded in and all I know, I woke up to a wet bed.

The memory which stuck with me longest, was that of Glen's girlfriend touching me and had me doing things to her. That was the first time I touched a woman and felt a woman on my mouth. Whenever I didn't do what she would say, she would pinch me. There was one time I went home with pinch marks on my skin and when my dad saw, it his response was, what did you do to piss Glen off?

I'm happy that, though things aren't perfect in your household, you were able to go to your parents and tell them about me. I know you did because your dad told me once, he came to me and said, can you believe Avery try chat shit about you touching her up? I think he wanted to believe you, but he didn't want to believe that his brother was Mr. Nasty. He wanted to keep acting like things were okay. I didn't even flinch when he said it. I had so many years of numbness. I wasn't fazed by the shit I was doing to you and that's the worst part.

The best thing that happened for both of us, was your parents walking in that evening. I'm happy it happened because it saved you from whatever would have happened. I was so drunk

Letters in Black

and high, anything was possible. Them walking in on us was good for me because I would have lost myself completely after that night if things had gone any farther.

You deserve to be happy. You deserve to have a smooth transition into adulthood. Push your parents to get you the therapy you need. If I could go back into the past and take it all back, I promise you, I would. As we can't make that return, I want you to fight for your happiness. You can become much more than a victim, the victim I forced you to be.

I don't want you to allow what I did to cause you to have men treat you as though you are less than valuable. You are a valuable Empress. You didn't have the greatest start, but remember, 'no' means 'no'. If he can't understand what the concept of 'no' is, don't give him any excuse or reason for your leaving. Just go. Don't return his calls. Don't respond to his text messages. Block his number. Cut all ties with him.

I was a dickhead. I don't even deserve your time right now. I don't really have much authority to be telling you what to do and what not to allow, I know this. It's just there are so many guys, men, Black men, who need to heal. They need to start working on healing before they can show that they are appreciative of your love and your time.

I started to reflect on who I was, what I was doing, why I did the shit I did and what I needed to do to escape that warped world, when Chloe emailed me. Glen died and Chloe emailed me. Her parents took her out of the situation we were in so they could protect their daughter. My parents, your grandparents, on the other hand, didn't do anything to protect me. They sent me back a little while longer and it changed from Glen's girl touching me, to him touching me and playing with me. Funny how that memory made itself known just now. I suppressed it for years, to the point I forgot.

I can't fully remember what happened, why I stopped going, but it stopped.

Chapter 9: **PERFECTIONISM**

Thursday, 16 June

Dear Black Man,

Perfection is a lie. Bad as it sounds, you will
never be perfect. There is no point in striving
for it. Bask in the moment of the process.
Allow the process to be your guide. Trust your
spirit. You know when everything is ready.
Don't talk yourself out of sharing what you've
worked so hard on.   5:32am

We all like the idea of everything being pristine, in its assumed place, in order. Any hint of chaos, or a slight trace of disorder would be too much for us to handle. This fantasy of an unflawed world is constantly being pushed on social media by influencers and brands. Hair set in place. Clothes, spick and span. Homes, clean block colours, black, white, beige, grey, brown. Equal numbers of throws and cushions. A utopian lifestyle to the T.

Almost all of the videos Ricardo viewed online, both intentionally and unintentionally, this is what he was fed. He knew better than to attempt emulating it all, but subconsciously this falsehood would endeavour to sneak into the way he lived. The decor in his living room centred around a monochrome theme, white walls, white rug, large white sofa set and a glass coffee table with contrasting black accents. He had black cushions, black candles, a large black analogue clock, and black framed pieces.

Nevertheless, this was something Ricardo had always been doing unconsciously throughout his life. His parents' home was just that, perfect. Colour schemes were vital, furniture sizes were key and he was taught to always present himself as very well put together. If he was going through a rough patch, he still dressed his face with a smile, pushing the tiredness to the back as his eyes would dare to show the sparkle he was infamously known for.

He committed himself to being the best for others. Outside of personal relationships and what he now coins as unfortunate sexual desires, he would ensure that others were very well looked after no matter the case. He rarely said no, at work he went above and beyond to give his team what they wanted and what he felt they needed; he denied himself to keep his managers on his side.

Though the relationship with his parents is frayed, there were moments they would ask him to drive them somewhere, or pay for something on their behalf, things they didn't need or was within their budget, and he would never tell them no. He took it to mean, they loved and appreciated him, though love may be a tad too strong a word to be used.

He needed to be in control of what was happening around him; it helped him to be at peace, if he were to take charge of the disorder around him. He found that the memories wouldn't flood in as much when he busied himself with other things.

What would have helped him over the years, was to learn that what he did to make others happy, was the thing that would kill him mentally. Without these lessons learned, he needed to be seen, accepted, flooded with compliments, and thank yous; these were all things he missed out on during his development as a child.

To the unknown, he was a natural giver. What everyone failed to realise was, he gave to receive. He wanted to receive anything remotely similar to being appreciated and loved. He made certain that everything he did was unquestionable. He thrived by living this way, but didn't realise, until rereading the text message, that his need for perfection was tangled within the realms of people pleasing.

"Alexa, play Spotify playlist Letters in Black."

Ricardo stretched and felt the tension in his muscles begin to soothe. His intention for today was to text Niyah with an apology and ask if they could potentially meet up once again. Writing the letters have been helpful for him, but what he had to say called for a face-to-face conversation, to clear things up, or so he led himself to believe. He didn't want to hide behind the phone sending text messages which could be read by her in a tone he wouldn't have used. He knew it wasn't going to be easy for her to sit with him, and he appreciated that this may just be one of the most difficult things she'd have to do to date, but a part of him really wanted to talk things through with her.

His body swayed as he rapped along with the lyrics to Kendrick Lamar's 'Alright' as it pumped through his speaker. Looking at his reflection, he observed his eyes, they were filled with pain. *Will I ever be alright?* He wanted to believe that someday, the pain, the burden would be lessened and he would find it easier to navigate through life.

As his reflection looked back at him, he figured today was as good as any to make his way to the gym. It had been some time since he was able to do any work on himself. Lat pulls would help to clear his mind.

His focus would be the weights, keeping his form, completing his reps. Rest. Repeat. Rest. Change machine. Seated rows. Pulling in strength, releasing the ache from his youth. Pulling in freedom, releasing the dreaded feeling of shame. Rest. Repeat. Rest. Change machine. Maybe add push ups to his drill. Strength. Work on physical strength.

He came back to reality upon hearing T.I.'s voice encouraging him to get back up. This playlist was far from his go to on a normal day, but the change was a requirement today. He was lacking motivation and if he knew one thing, it was that this playlist was prescribed specifically to get him moving.

Morning cuz. Hope you've been well. I know things didn't go too well last time we met, but just wondering if we could try again you know. Stay bless.

His eyes ran over the words on his screen as they willed him to press send. It wasn't fair to ask Niyah to subject herself to this, he knew this, but amends were required. Contemplating whether to send the messageor not didn't last long. It was interrupted by a text from an unknown number.

I'm sure you would have been okay with an email, but I hate to send them from my phone, and all I'm doing is saying hi. So, hey twin! What's good? What's new? How's life treating you? We need to link up. Love, Chloe.

Ricardo had one word which popped up without thought, shit. He'd not gotten in touch with her for months now and his last message was left in drafts. Chloe was the one person he feared contacting so to be asked to meet up was a lot for him. He wasn't sure how he would face her with the secrets he held onto for dear life.

And good morning. I don't even know if you're up yet. If you weren't awake and are up because of me, I'm sorry haha. If you were awake, I feel no shame.

Ricardo laughed as he read her message. Though worried, he appreciated the light heartedness in it. His day would officially begin once he got through his morning routine, brushing his teeth, washing his face, having a shower. These were nothing but crucial.

He couldn't be one of those people whose breath would do nothing but fight wars with the nostrils of other commuters. Or those who forgot what it ever meant to restart the day in a good manner, clean pits.

Before jumping into the shower, he dropped Chloe a quick text, acknowledging her, something to let her know he wasn't attempting to ignore her. Laughter erupted from his core; this healing world was more difficult than he was expecting. There was a part of him that wished it was a path left unventured but it needed to happen, at some point in life, and, apparently, this was the time.

With water cascading down his body, Ricardo's mind pondered more and more about texting Niyah. To try again. Attempting to show how sorry he was, sounded like a marvellous idea. On the other hand, to text her asking for this, would be to force her hand, force her to see the one who robbed her of her values, her identity, her truth. It wasn't fair and he knew this. *Just because she's an adult don't mean I can do this to her*, he muttered.

Memories, thoughts about the future, images of what could be, surged through in his mind. Fist pounding the wall, he tried his hardest to fight what was becoming an intricate web of self-doubt, broken confidence, heightened anxiety, a deep wave of sadness, and an ocean of depression.

Questions of 'why me' pricked and poked, prodded and pulled at his mind. As far as he had been concerned, he was doing well, he was understanding all, he could see that healing wasn't a journey with a final destination. But he wanted to fix what went wrong. He couldn't go back and make better choices and, in the present, it didn't make sense to try to coerce anyone to forgive him for his sins.

This is the face of healing he could not have prepared for.

"Oh wow! A voice! This is what you sound like these days?" She mocked.

"Raaa! We aint chat in years and this is the greeting I get? Where is the love rude girl?"

"Yo! This is what you get! You stopped replying to my emails. You have never returned my calls or my texts. At least I'm not cussing you out!"

"This is true." Ricardo agreed. The reception from Chloe could have been different. For her to have called him after he disappeared on her, she could have said something worse to him. "What you telling me cuz?"

"You tell me, you're the one who went dark!" She mocked. "And you can take your hand from off your chest. You are not Will Smith and this is not Bel Air."

"Shut up fam! Acting like you know me!"

"Was it a lie though? Over there grinning teeth."

Chloe found her way in. She was happy to hear the way pleasure made an entrance in his voice. Before he stopped replying to her, there was something about the way his replies seemed to be carefully crafted, a treasure map of sorts, yet she couldn't find the treasure, they were more of a car boot sale.

"Tell me you're not over there with teeth shining white?"

"'llow me fam." Ricardo was grateful to share in this light-hearted nature Chloe offered. A blessing in disguise after the morning he faced. The way his chest pushed itself upwards, the way it deflated, he knew this was how freedom felt. There was no iciness, no forced softness, no broken glass to tippytoe around. His laugh was careless. It was no longer bouncing off padded walls. Instead, it flailed about, crashing into atoms and elements that writhed in pain. It sought out radicals that new bonds could be formed, that they would push aside worries and instead live contently within him.

Seconds turned to minutes and the minutes became hours pushing all thoughts of headed to the gym to the back of Ricardo's mind. But, as Jamaican's loved to say, trouble nuh set like rain, he couldn't have seen this one coming. There was no forecast to inform him that he needed to control the rate at which his heart would run.

"How did you know?"

"I've got a friend called Christine. We've known each other for some years now, went uni together. She was telling me about her dickhead brother-in-law one day, made no mention of his name and I wasn't interested. I've never met her husband and she doesn't post pictures of him online, that says a lot. He doesn't want her putting up pictures of him like say he is some show pony. Her words not mine."

Breathe in. Breathe out. Breathe in. Breathe out. Like innocence, good things do not last long. They get robbed. They get snatched.

"Long and short of it, we were having a full-blown heart to heart and she broke down. She told me about the night they came home and caught her in-law. Everything in her broke because she had never believed her daughter. I was fuming when she told me. Inside, I raged. What mother doesn't believe her child?"

He could tell that her jaw was tight. Her voice was calm, but he could feel the anger brewing in each word. She was a hurricane waiting to happen.

"I allowed her to vent. I let her get everything of her chest and slip of the tongue, she called your name, and David's. It couldn't have been coincidence. How many Ricardo Bennetts does England host? Ricardo Bennett with an older brother called David Bennett? And yeah, I said Christine, didn't I? That's the name I call her, but her name is really Eva, Eva-Christine."

Breathe in. Breathe out. Breathe in. Breathe out.

Chloe sniffled and under her breath counted ten...nine...eight...seven...six...five...four...three...two...one.

"I can't lie, I was so vex when I found out. Even before confirming that it was you. I was vex. What vex me more was the fact that we were sending emails back and forth and you never used any of those to-"

"I didn't know how to."

"But I thought we were open with each other?"

"You were open with me. I couldn't find the words to tell you the truth without you hating me."

The line went still. Ricardo felt the walls closing in on him but feared saying that he could no longer go any further with this conversation. Knowing but not understanding that he was on the verge of having a panic attack, he continued to repeat *breathe in, breathe out. Breathe in. Breathe out.* His repetition growing louder, faster, Chloe recognised what was happening and stepped in to help her cousin. Reassuring him that she was there for him. Encouraging him to take slow, deep breaths. Having gone through this herself, she knew to remain calm on his behalf.

Once Chloe was able to help him through it, they said their goodbyes, and Ricardo with determination, set out to the gym. He took a scenic route instead of getting into his car. He needed to be outside, the confinement of his car was likely to trigger another attack. He needed the fresh air.

The world around him buzzed with vendors shouting out what they were selling, pensioners chatting as they sat in outdoor seated areas of their favourite cafés, kids out of uniform, his guess, Year 11s or Sixth Formers, exam season upon them, having not had to sit formal exams in the past two year, he could envision their anxieties. The buzz was warm and friendly, it encouraged him to restore inner peace. Though he had headphones on, there was nothing playing, giving him the chance to listen in on conversations as he walked by.

Cars would drive by playing old school hits, 21 Seconds by So Solid Crew, Always on Time by Ja Rule, Welcome to Jamrock by Damian Marley. There was no doubt that the summer sun changed the mood of people and always brought music. He was able to appreciate summer in South London because it emulated the vibrancy of Jamaica, not in its entirety, but with enough Jamaicans in South, home was on his doorstep.

He put his pin in at the entrance and was greeted with the musk from gymgoers past and present. He didn't miss this, but he was on a mission and had no time to give too much of his energy to the disturbance the stenches wanted to cause on his insides. He still had his plan, get some lat pulls done, do some seated rows, push ups, bicep curls, pull ups, dips. He was determined to work through his cycle. This cycle. He needed to clear his mind, regain control. He was out of sorts and had to fix this before his mental health spiralled. This was all too familiar for him and he regrets having previously allowed his personal life to worsen, and that he did not get to speak with anyone who would have been able to help him.

He wished for a male friend in whom he could confide. One who would not make fun of his situation, but one who would understand the detriment he faced. He knew that had the shoe been on the other foot and a friend wanted to confide in him, he would mock their pain, and laugh at their trauma. There was little emotional intelligence in him then. He needed to have these conversations with another man, another Black man. The Black world he found, was quick to highlight the struggles of Black women, but never spoke about the mental health and healing of a Black man. They knew Black women had huge struggles with their mental health and the White world wasn't kind to them, so these Black women needed to always be on guard. But on the flip side, their male counterparts were left out to dry and no one was caring enough to bring them in when the weather conditions would change.

Black men were always ridiculed, ever since they were able to voice their concerns. They were called 'men' from a young age; unlike Black women, they weren't able to grow up and enjoy childhood. They instead had to brace themselves to become men, and if their father left their homes, they automatically became the man of the house to protect their mothers and provide for their family. It was laughable, though painful, and sad, because some of the guys on streets started selling while they were in their teens, some even younger because they wanted to alleviate the stress from their mothers. Those on the outside would crucify them for the moves they chose to make, but they didn't understand that these boys, were 'men' the minute their fathers left the home. Ricardo's father never left, but, growing up, he was always told he was a man. He was certain his boys went through a similar thing at home when they too were younger.

Chapter 10: **REREADS**

118 Elm Tree Road
Lewisham
England
SE13 5SQ
16 – Jun – 2022

Dear Niyah,

I thought about texting you this morning, typed the text and everything, all that was left was for me to press send, but I couldn't. I was adamant that we had to meet up again. Try again, so I could explain myself. I feel bad for everything that I did, and, in my mind, it's like, I was expecting because you're an adult, I was expecting that you'd be able to go through sitting with me and hearing what I had to say. When in all fairness, that's me opening up your old wounds and forcing you to forgive me so I can move on with my life.

It's a shame that I had reached out to you before to invite you to sit down with me. Don't get me wrong, I appreciate you for coming, but it was a selfish move. I should have known better because one time when Chloe emailed me about our Uncle Glen, she was saying she couldn't come back to Lewisham because it would be too much for her.

What I never told you properly, was that our Uncle Glen, mine and Chloe's uncle that is, he used to get me to touch her and got us to whine up with each other. I can't remember what the touch up thing used to be like, not in full, but I know it wasn't meant to have happened. He used to tell me no one would believe me if I told them, and was very degrading. Chloe was never seen as his niece; I don't think I was ever seen as his nephew. With the way he used to tell me, man nuh fi fraid ah di pussy, and force me to touch her, I feel like he used to see her as just that. Pussy. Not young, nor old, but just pussy.

I used to also watch my dad beat up my mum. He was sick, this man used to get me and David to watch. I learnt how to manipulate females from a young age and in my mind,

Letters in Black

you lot were just here to be touch up and that's what happened. I manipulated you, lied to you, then started doing to you what I was taught to do to Chloe. I'm sure by time I was 12 I should have known better, but this brain was wired in a weird way and I don't think I had enough control over myself back then.

I was never able to properly talk to my parents about Glen and it was something they even knew, but they kept sending me over to the man's yard. I was never trusting of David so I couldn't talk to him either. So when it came to what I did to you, I promise, I wanted to talk to someone about it. I knew it was wrong, but I didn't have anyone I trusted. You'd even think I would have said it to one of my friends in school, but I was never ever 100% real with them.

That was a secret I held on to and wanted to hold onto until my grave. Never thought I would ever reopen this box, but here we are. If I could go back and change the past, I would. If I could take back the hurt and pain I put you through, I would.

I wish I never brought harm to you. I think I'm getting to understand a little more about trauma and how deep-seated it is. I'm not all the way there with it, but I'm learning about it. I'm getting to see how it causes a person to eff up in their life and I know sorry won't suffice, but just hoping you can accept my apology. I'm also still working on forgiving myself for everything I've done.

I love you for your strength. Thanks for having met up with me after what I did. Thank you for forgiving me, if you have. If you've not been able to, I can understand why, because I don't think I've even forgiven my uncle and the man is dead.

Look after yourself cuz,

Ricardo.

118 Elm Tree Road
Lewisham
England
SE13 5SQ
19-May-2020

Dear Niyah,

I did some things in the past that wasn't ever right. I treated you in a way I shouldn't have. I wish I could have this conversation with you face to face but I can't even think of where to start with it all.

My uncle died last year and when I learned of his death, so much started brewing in me. To piece everything together, my emotions, my thoughts about myself when he died, thoughts about who I was when everything happened as a kid and even about how I was when he was arrested and throughout his court case, most difficult thing I had to do. I couldn't do it. I didn't. I allowed his death to control me. That's when I let go of living. I didn't go to the funeral. It didn't make sense. The man was a monster. He really carried out some heinous acts and there was no way I could celebrate him. And that's how I fell out with my parents. My dad cussed me, talked about family values when he himself didn't know what that was. My mum stood by him like a lost puppy agreeing with him but this man battered her for years. Nothing, no amount of money, no amount of guilt trip from family, would get me at that man's burial.

His death ate away at me though. I started drinking heavily, missed bare days off work. Messed up in my relationship at the time, started treating my girl a way, wasn't showing up to appointments with her.

I have a son by the way.

Letters in Black

Yeah, I wasn't going to appointments with her, her scans and all of that to do with her pregnancy. I was ghosting the woman I thought I loved. I think I still love her. I don't even know if I know what love is! My uncle died when she was six months pregnant, baby born in August. Remember when I rocked up to your office?

She doesn't know anything about my uncle and when I was adamant that my brother would never babysit, she would look at me like I was mad. I was. I wanted us to move out of London, moving out of England sounded great as well. I didn't want us to be around my family. I knew what I went through and didn't want my son subjected to that. Fully ironic right?

I was drinking so much. When D asked me to stay with Avery, there's a part of me that knew I should have said no, but, I was more concerned with not wanting anyone to know the depths of what I was going through. The weed. The liquor. That was the lowest day of my life. Lowest of baby girl's as well. My own niece. The shit I wanted my son to be protected from, I did to my niece. I still feel sick thinking about what I did, but, it happened you know.

How a man destroys his niece is beyond me. Sometimes I don't think I know the man I was. The one who caused harm to Avery. I was always a risk but no-one knew about it. Come to think of it, did you ever tell your parents about the shit I put you through when we were younger?

I never thought of it before. If they knew, what did they do to protect you? When did they find out? If they knew, did they tell my parents? I don't know if I'd prefer my parents knowing and hadn't done anything about it or them just not knowing. I don't even know which is the lesser of the two evils.

I wish I knew how to properly communicate with you last year. I honestly needed help, but didn't know the right words to use to ask for help so the idiot I was ended up fabricating shit about wanting to do the same to someone else's child.

I guess I've spent time asking myself why I did that. Of all scenarios I could have come up with, that's the one I chose. Something like that should have gotten me locked up. Speaking of lock up, I'm grateful to have had a second chance to become a better man, but I guess it's a slap in the face for you and Avery to know that no charges were pressed. David didn't even get a restraining order against me.

Guilt for what I did gnawed at me night after night.

I have a cousin, her name is Chloe, she went through some things right, when Glen died, she emailed me out of the blue, I aint seen her for years and, she emailed me when he died. Her emails made me feel like a voodoo doll being poked. I know that's a Hollywood kind of thing, but that's how it felt to be real. I felt as though a spell was cast and I was walking with demons, day and night. I lost hours of sleep across countless nights. There were days I didn't make it to work and when I did, I was barely alert. I was a big mess last year and I don't know how people tolerated me.

I hope one day you can find it in your heart to forgive me.

Ricardo.

Letters in Black

118 Elm Tree Road
Lewisham
England
SE13 5SQ
19-May-2020

Hey Tamara,

How are you? How's little man? He should be about 7 months now, right? I did you dirty and I'm so sorry. I'm not proud of what I've done and I hope that at some point in life you'll be able to forgive me.

You were a good factor in my life but I shut you out at the most important time. I hid a key part of my life from you because, which woman really wants to be with a man whose sex tricks are remnants of forced lessons he learned as a kid?

I went through the most when I was younger and that's why I didn't want Jace to ever be around my brother. I don't know what kind of man he really is; I know he's a teacher and all, but I can't trust anyone. Me, myself, I'm a sheg. I used to touch up my cousin when we were younger, then I did the same to Avery. Everything was flipped upside down last year. Police got involved and everything. For me, there was a blessing knowing that no charges were pressed and police didn't even warrant it all as anything much anyway. It's not right, I know, but for me, it's a real shot at becoming better for myself first and everyone else next.

When my uncle died, that's when things got bad for me. I got emails from my cousin Chloe which shook my world, turning things upside down. So much of my past came up. I started to feel inadequate, didn't think I could do right by you and our son. I didn't want to be in his life and turn out to be a piece of shit father. I think it's better to not be around, instead of being around and being shit.

I hope you haven't minded me sending you money over the past months for little man. Did you name him Jace in the end? Who does he get his looks from? I hope one day I can get to come around and see him, get to know him. I don't know if you'd want to introduce me to him as his father or your friend, maybe an old friend?

I know he can't too understand a lot right now, but whenever you talk about me, please don't make him hate me. You don't have to tell him that I'm the greatest around, not like I am anyway. Just asking that you don't make him hate me. I would have love to have been there for my boy, but the way life's set, it wasn't happening.

I'm going to work on being the best for my son though I'm not physically in his life. I don't want to ruin him. I want him to get to know himself without losing bits of his identity without me tainting it with the little understanding of manhood that I have.

I'm sorry Tammy. You were nothing but good to me and I flaked. You deserve better than me. I was doing the bare minimum because I didn't know how to give much else. One day I'll become a better man, I'm sure of it, only thing is, that might be too late, won't it? Would you even consider taking me back when I change? Is there still room for me in your heart?

Thanks for teaching me what love was to feel like. You knew I was withholding information, but you never stopped showing up for me. You continued to love. You gave me what I needed so I could believe in love. You did what you could until you could go no further and I appreciate you for that.

At the start of our relationship, I told you I wasn't looking for much because commitment scared me. I even thought you were crazy to be with me for so long, just chilling, caring, not asking for anything of me. I didn't get it. I didn't get that to love meant showing up. You showed up. You didn't stop showing up. You kept turning up. You were patient.

Letters in Black

I'm sorry for taking your kindness, your love, and ruining it. You wanted what was best for me, but I held on to the worst part of me because I didn't want to lose you. Now look.

Anyway, I hope you're good. I wish I could be there to help you out on those sleepless nights and do my duty. I chickened out and became a timewaster, the dad you didn't want for our son, the dad we discussed I wasn't to be. I agreed with you on how to make his life work, but now, I've left. I know the money alone isn't good enough.

I'm sorry. I hope you can forgive me one day Tammy.

Ricky.

118 Elm Tree Road
Lewisham
England
SE13 5SQ
19-May-2020

Jace,

Little man. I'm sorry I can't be the father you need in your life. Your mother may never allow me back in and for that, I take full responsibility. I should have never stepped out on her when she was carrying you.

Your mother is an exceptional woman. She is patient, she was patient with me. I know that's contradictory because I doubt, she will take me back, but she has to do what's best for both of you. Being patient with someone doesn't mean you sit around and wait for them to come back after they've left and walked away. Being patient is giving them the space they need, give them an allowance, room to make mistakes, room to grow. She did what she could, she waited, she allowed me to go through my hell, but I chose wrongly and I walked out.

Your mother is kind. She has gone out of her way so many times for the ones she loves and cares about. I'm sure if I was honest with her, she would have done the same for me. I stole that opportunity from her. I should have trusted her and whatever outcome life had for me then. I want you to trust your mother, trust that she has your best interest at heart and will show you what true compassion is. Don't let your ego get in the way.

I should have done better for you. I should have stuck around but I was too afraid. I was scared that my past was going to affect your future, and that's why I left. Now, in hindsight, my fear did manifest itself when I walked out of your mother's life. The moment I

Letters in Black

started pulling back, making myself less visible in her life, being there for her while you were growing inside her, that's when my fears began to unfold.

I can't take anything back right now. I made my bed and have to sleep in it. But I want you to know this had nothing to do with you. Don't go out there seeking a father in your friends. Be mindful of the friends you keep.

Always tell your mother whenever you're hurt. She's your first friend. She is there to protect you. She is there to help you to feel better, help to take the pain away. Always remember to tell her whenever you're hurt. If someone hurts you, makes you feel uncomfortable, tell her. She needs to know.

I want you to be a better child than I was, a better teenager than I was and a better man than I could ever be. Your stepfather, as long as he isn't hurting you, trust him. Don't ever turn around and tell him that he's not your dad when he disciplines you. He is a father figure, a Black male figure you need in your life. Your mother has a good head on her shoulders, I believe she will not allow anyone near you if they will put you in danger, so trust him.

You may have my blood, but, as much as I don't want to even say this, it doesn't mean I'm your father. The only thing I've taught you, by not being around, is that when problems arise you should run away. That's not a lesson I want you to hold on to. Before sitting down to write, I saw something which said a real man doesn't leave in difficult times. I think I can agree with it. I want you to be a better man than me. One who doesn't leave in difficult times, instead, problem solves and works on solutions.

Look after yourself little man.
I love you.
Your dad,
Ricardo.

Ricardo looked at the letter in his hand. His son would now be two years and one month old, but he's never met him. He's seen Tamara on odd occasions, but never with him. She was making it through as a single mother, always thankful for the money she received and he thought this was the reason she never spoke about taking him to court.

He was honest with her about his pay and had researched how much to pay for child support. As a project manager in his bank, with what he was paid, the child maintenance calculator figured he would be liable to pay £118.56 a week or £513.40 a month for his son. This wasn't something he discussed with Tamara, not when they were together as a hypothetical situation, not when he decided to start paying. He knew it still wasn't enough and he lived a comfortable life, so paying more than what the calculator suggested was easy for him to do. He wondered if his mother left his father, in the event, he didn't pay child support what would have happened, how she would have reacted?

There was a sinking feeling in Ricardo, one which threatened to pull his heart into the pits of his stomach. Nauseated, he held onto the letter, thinking about the life he left behind. In his mind a vision played out of him laughing with his son as he taught him how to kick a ball. Or flying him around the sitting room making aeroplane sounds while Tamara held onto her anxieties praying, he would not let him fall. *Shall we get him a dog?* He heard himself ask as they laid in bed snuggled up with Jace between them. *Or do you want to try for another?* He'd say as she made out as though she was going to hit him. Then she would look at him and say *we can get him a dog when he learns how to look after himself because I'm not doing no pooperscoops.*

The vision brought a warm smile to his face, but his heart cried. He wanted to be the man who was there for his child, he wanted to be a better father than his father was. Instead, he removed himself from the equation because he didn't trust that Tamara would have supported him. Maybe she wouldn't have, but, who is to tell, had he been trans parent with her, maybe she would have helped him through his ordeal. Ricardo's thoughts were interrupted by the forceful vibration of his phone as No Role Models by J.Cole spilled out. Hesitantly he answered as the number on his screen was unfamiliar to him.

"Hello?"

"Greetings King. It's Stanley."

"What's good King?" Ricardo feigned an attempt at sounding confident in knowing who it was.

"It's S.Dot bruv", Stanley laughed.

"Raa! Swear down?" Ricardo exclaimed.

"Yeah fam! Been a while my G. What's new man?"

"Brudda, I don't even know. Wah gwaan wid you?"

"I got a family, 2 youths and a beautiful wife. I've got a business, working with Black boys at risk of joining gangs. Bought a place in Jamaica and running an Airbnb out there. Yeah man that's my life right now."

"You're going on good brudda. I'm happy for you."

"Thanks King."

Stanley was always the friend Ricardo had whom he would catch up with, ever so often. They met back in college, good old CTK, countless debates in their Philosophy classes. Stanley managed to maintain good grades at college while keeping his rep on the road. The last thing Ricardo knew about him was that he had gone university out of the UK; his parents didn't like the direction he was headed though he had the grades.

The two caught up on life over the past years and Ricardo listened in on how life panned out for Stanley, surprised that he returned to life in the UK. Ricardo inquired about the relationship Stanley had with his family, what it was like and what he took from the parenting strategies his parents used when he was younger to implement into what he did.

Ricardo listened keenly, wanting to take lessons from Stanley to incorporate into his parenting style, not that there was one. From what he was hearing he knew that Stanley was doing all that he could for his children.

With the past Stanley had, Ricardo understood why he started his business. He had great insight into what life was like within gangs, how dangerous it was, not only for the boys, but also for their families.

Having been close to putting his parents and siblings at risk as a teen, Stanley was able to learn from his past and use these lessons to prevent young men from ending up behind bars or in the grave.

The dreaded question came, washing over Ricardo with waves of disappointment and guilt. Nevertheless, he found himself saying, "I have a yute, two years old but I've never met him."

"Swear? How comes?"

"I was on a madness man. One of my uncles died and then I went on a mad one-"

"Shit, sorry to hear about your uncle fam."

"It's cool. He needed to die man. This man was the reason for a lot of shit I went through as a yute."

"What do mean by that?"

Ricardo laughed nervously and shared stories from his past with Stanley, pausing momentarily, punctuating his stream of thoughts with an uncomfortable chuckle.

"Yo bro, I'm sorry to hear that man. I can only imagine how that played out in later life."

"I'm still working through it man."

"How have you been doing that?"

Letters. Writing letters that I will never send. Was his first thought but he wasn't sure if this was something he could share. His wound felt too fresh for him to allow his defences to fall too close to the ground. He still suckled the fear of being judged and his answer became "I've been giving myself time and room to feel my emotions. I have to deconstruct thoughts like 'men don't cry', so I can push past that block and allow myself to release years of pain through tears."

"That's a good start man. Take it a day at a time. I don't know if you ever heard your grandparents say this, but, is not same day leaf drop in water it rotten. Whatever you do, never forget to stay true to you brudda."

As both said their goodbyes, gratitude filled Ricardo. This was the first time in his history that he has been able to be honest with another Black man without being ridiculed. Ricardo was surprised about how light he felt after their conversation. Lifting his head, a broad smile crept across his face, divorcing the doubts and fears he was having as he read the letters. *Jah you really come through in the darkest hours,* he thought.

"Alexa play Jah by My Side by Tony Rebel." He requested of the only woman he'd in recent times allowed to live with him. This song had never meant much to him until this moment.

The call he had, helped him to see past the guilt that he cloaked himself in when reading his letters. The biggest part of his healing started when he sat down to write his very first letter. These letters gave him the space he needed to pour his heart out without being criticised.

Chapter 11: **FORGIVE**

Friday, 17 June

Dear Black Man,

We are graced with life as a wonderful present.
We are granted opportunities to right our
wrongs. What we do with these opportunities
will impact the path we take. Don't do
something that will overthrow your peace.   5:32am

Queen Shayla! Blessings to you. This rings true to me,
thanks for the reminder, I appreciate it and you.

Wishing you well today. I hope your day is filled with
the blessings you deserve to be showered in. Thank
you for being you. My world has been in need. Bless up
5:50am   Empress.

Awww thank you! Why are you awake? Are you
not on leave?   5:51am

I'm used to waking up early, so sadly for me, I'm awake.
Gonna head gym though.
5:55am

Yaaaas! Go win in that gym! I'm going back to
sleep lol   5:57am

5:57am   What? Why? Aint you got work?

Mental health day :smilley face: 5:58 am

5:58am   Come again?

I gave myself a mental health day. Work is pure
stress nowadays and I don't have capacity for
their bullshit. Not today anyway.   6:01 am

In other words, you've called in sick? I hear that with
6:02am   not wanting to deal with their bull though.

Spot on. I'll return to work on Monday and that
way I don't need to get doctor's note.   6:03am

6:03am   Smart! Rest up Shay.

Thanks x   6:03am

It was an easier morning for Ricardo. The exchange between himself and Shayla, followed by using the gym in a different manner helped him to tweak the way he was viewing things. He was able to maintain a clear mind through to midday and took advantage of the weather by sitting out in a park with a novel.

He didn't always find novels entertaining but he got wind of Th1rt3en by Steve Cavanagh recommended by a booktoker, @zthereader. It's a book Z enjoyed but don't see enough of this book on booktok. When he saw the video, he had to add it to his favourites just because he knew he would forget. He wasn't brave enough to reach out to her but was beyond grateful for her thoughts.

The plot was genius. He was certain if the main character was real, he would applaud him for his brilliance. Ricardo was used to plots which had folks working in the bank who helped with the robbery, but to have a character infiltrate the judicial system, to sit in on a case about the crimes he committed, this got Ricardo excited. He wasn't that far in, but he was sucked in deeply enough.

The cool of the air danced on his arms. He, like everyone else who was no stranger to the weather in London, knew the essentials required when leaving home, and was grateful he followed his mind taking one of his hoodies with him. Goosebumps made an appearance over his arms, which caused him to reach for his hoodie and happened to see her in that moment. He didn't know what to think of it. He wanted to believe that it was coincidental. More than anything, he wanted to believe that this was a sign for him to reach out to her. Though he wasn't thinking about making contact when talking about her yesterday, the thought of it in this present state, felt like a good idea.

He looked at her in the distance, her body being hugged tightly by the brown dress she wore complementing her warm cinnamon skin and hour glass figure. A familiar sadness crept up as he recognised the converses worn on her feet. He could remember the morning as clear as day. He snuck out of bed an hour before he knew she would be awake, got her present out of his car, along with the balloons he bought. He was giddy, he was never with a woman long enough to get presents for her birthday, or Christmas, or an anniversary. He would conveniently break up with these women before any celebratory event would make itself known. He cooked Tamara a hearty breakfast, laid out an outfit for her on the chair in the room, tiptoeing around while setting the balloons down, had a shower and caught some of Tom and Jerry while she slept.

He could hear the excited shriek from the bedroom and listened for her footsteps to race down the hall. Her face was brightly lit by a joy he was never able to bring to anyone before. His heart melted in the moment. Her glow was a vortex to peace. He held her in his arms, whispering happy birthdays in her ear, telling her how much he loved her.

Today, she wore exhaustion on her body, her shoulders tensed. She dragged her body as though it were a hassle to take with her. In her left hand she pulled a child's scooter beside her. Ricardo looked around expecting to see a little boy running towards her, but, to his disappointment, there wasn't a child in sight.

"I can't do this alone... what do you mean? You are barely ever around... tell me the last time you've been home... no, it's been 2 months. Two long months... No! I don't miss your sex but your children miss you... I know you're doing this for us but you said... you said you would leave. I fell pregnant with Brayton and you said you would leave before I gave birth."

Ricardo listened in on the conversation an unknown female was having, he assumed with her husband. The oscillation of her tone, the dynamics of her volume, the crescendo and diminuendo, he could feel the stress she was left with. He could feel Tamara's stress she walked with across the mini bridge in the Kyoto Garden.

"Savannah cried before she slept last night. She asked if you no longer love her… I lied to her, told her yes… it was a lie because I don't even know if you know what it means to love your children anymore."

Her voice vibrated as her cadence fluctuated. Ricardo felt broken as the trembles in her voice became prominent with soft sobs. It dawned on him that his son would ask Tamara questions about his love and she too would have to create a reason for his absence. His past self, thought it was for the best. But, with time, with life, he has learnt that his absence would create a tornado of untamed emotions in his son. Tamara could do all she could for him, but she would never be able to replace, or replicate what Ricardo could be for their son. She would never be able to fill that void. He could understand now what Kendrick Lamar meant in Father Time. How eerie it was to be experiencing this weight of time shortly after listening to that particular song.

He blew the air which rested in his lungs, shaking his head. This joke he felt life was trying to give was dark and there wasn't a fibre within his body which was willing to share in it; nothing in him wanted to laugh.

I'm sorry for leaving you to take care of little man on your own. I wish I could change the past. Let me know what more I can do to help, I'm not expecting that you will want me to come around and take him, but if you want me to pay for a babysitter or anything, let me know.

He hit send before he could spend any time overthinking his decision. Within a minute of hitting send, his phone vibrated. It was Tamara.

I want you to meet your son. I stuck with the name we chose for him, Jace. I want him to get to know his father and I want for you to take him sometimes. I'm tired Ricardo. I love him but it's hard doing this alone. He's got so much energy, it's crazy. He's at nursery 3 days a week, but it means I'm having to leave work to get him and when at home with him, trying to work, it's hard.

Eyes glued to his phone, he started to question whether he was ready for this commitment. He didn't know anything about being a father. Would him being in his son's life now bring harm? Was he able to be a father?

Yes, you left, that can't be changed. I'm not even mad at you about it anymore. I just wish you would have been honest with me about everything and trusted me to stand with you to help you work through. But you left. I just want you to promise me one thing, if you do start forming a bond with Jace and shit starts to hit the fan, trust me to be there to understand. Trust me to support you in fatherhood. He needs his father in his life. He doesn't need a runner.

Ricardo felt a dark portal being opened wanting to suck him in. He wanted to make that promise, but it wasn't her he didn't trust, it was himself. He couldn't trust that he would get to a point in his life where he would not run, in hopes to protect his son.

I can't lie, I can't even make that promise right about now. I don't wanna make that promise and then break it. What if I don't know how to be a good father to him? I'd love to be in my boy's life, but I don't even know how to. I'm still tryna work on healing and there is a lot I need to heal from. I'll be happy to meet up with you and him, but don't know when I would be able to take him from you.

Healing is never a complete package. It comes in dribs and drabs. Some days will be better than others, but the most important thing is being committed to becoming better. Back in the days you used to read self-help books to be a better man, I mocked you, but in hindsight I've been seeing the benefits of those books. I can't say if you're ready to be a father, but I believe you will always work towards being a good father for our son.

The last time was the day he scared her. The day she trusted him a little less. The day she suspected he was hiding something from her. The last time was the day he realised he couldn't trust himself to be comfortable around her for his comfort would bring complacency.

Chapter 12: **MORLEY'S**

"Have you ever been to therapy?"

"I tried but it wasn't for me."

"What makes you say that?"

"Had a white man who never seemed to give a damn about a Black man who needed help."

"Wrong fit. I hear that. You know if you wanted to try again you could just do a search online for Black counsellors right? There are Black male counsellors out there too."

"Maybe some time in the future. The only thing this man heard is what got police on me. Well, that plus my cousin went to them first."

"What do you mean?"

"Look yeah, when you're a damn fool tryna get help and don't know how to properly ask for it, you fabricate shit in hopes that it will get you in the door."

Both simultaneously placed hands in their pockets looking up at the vivacious red sign above the door, Morley's, South London's infamous chicken shop. At the end of the school day teenagers would spill out of the doors waiting to be served, two-piece chicken and chips was always a good go to. To gain the attention of staff, 'bossman' would escape from the mouths of these young people in a rush, sometimes with a friend keeping watch to see if their bus was on the way.

During their days at CTK, McDonald's was more the go to than Morley's. It was a good place for Secondary School and College students to link up. There weren't a lot of fights back then, but a lot of days it would be rowdy, this was the atmosphere Lewisham was accustomed to. It was the culture and adults didn't seem to be bothered with the happenings so long as the yobs kept to themselves.

"Memories! Wah gwaan bossman?" Stanton spoke to the South Asian gentleman behind the counter. It was rare to walk into a Morley's shop and see a Black, or even white person working there, they were largely ran by South Asians. It was their world and everyone in South London was okay with it.

They tended, similar to this guy, to respond in the slang adopted by Londoners with 'wah gwaan'. It was accepted, there were no questions or rows about cultural appropriation. It was a known and accepted fact that the business people they were, knew the dialect and would connect with their customers using said dialect.

"Two-piece chicken and chips, but no drumsticks, and can I get a portion of flat wings." Stanton spoke comfortably making his order, looking behind the 'bossman' in the fridge, "let me get a Ting as well. How much is that?

"Nine pound sixty-nine".

"That's that inflation life fam." Ricardo laughed.

"Never thought I would see the day that Morley's got expensive dawg."

Ricardo placed his order and both men reminisced on what it was like for them growing up in Lewisham. The nicknames of schools, 'pum pum palace', 'hoes on the hill' and the other names they couldn't remember. They laughed about the time when being a bowcat was frowned upon even though a number of guys fit the description. Their era in Lewisham wasn't much different from today's where there is still a huge issue with postcode wars, youngsters repping 'ends' because that's what they've been taught to do. Just as when they were growing up and found it difficult to go into certain areas knowing trouble would be looming.

There was a bittersweet nostalgic air looming above them. It was great to reconnect with someone who understood their past, but it hurt to know how deep rooted, beyond the house, beyond family, the disrespect for females was. Young boys referred to young women based on their school's nicknames.

"Tell me about this counsellor you were seeing, what happened?"

Ricardo averted his eyes from the box in his hand and thought about the fateful day he arrived at his counsellor's office. He was an older white man with a bald head, and a gut. He resembled Ricardo's English teacher from Secondary School. He wore a small pair of reading glasses on the top of his head. His shirt was a size too small and you could see the white it was to be, had faded into an off looking yellow. His trousers looked as though they were coming loose, had he gotten up from his seat, they may have fallen from his body.

He had barely looked up at Ricardo when he directed him to take a seat. He failed to create a warmth in the room causing Ricardo to feel uncomfortable, but he still brought himself to telling this man before him the lie he told his cousin in hopes she would see to him. He was not made aware that his counsellor would report him to the police. He divulged his past to the man who wasn't bothered about how this had impacted him. He didn't ask any questions to allow Ricardo to discuss the lie he told Niyah. It was a torturous hour for Ricardo, but he persevered.

He was never able to book a follow-up appointment with the counsellor, his assistant was always adamant that he was never available on the days Ricardo chose. She also carefully avoided telling Ricardo the days his counsellor could potentially have a slot to see him.

Days later two police officers turned up to his apartment, not thinking anything of it, he opened his door and when asked to step outside, he did. He would never be able to say he was street smart at this point, had he known better, he wouldn't have stepped outside.

Though they took him in for questioning, he explained that when he visited Niyah's place of work, he fibbed solely to speak to her. He told them about the death of his uncle and the wrath his uncle placed upon his life as a child.

Ricardo somehow maintained his composure and retold this story to Stanley, surprising himself as he shared this story, one he had never divulged this to his brother.

"Fam you been through the most init."

"Yeah man!"

"Blessings to you man. You've done well. Some man would have turned out worse and you've even been working on moving past that. You've been doing well."

"Thanks brudda. You've done well too. Your work is needed for these yutes today. They need someone who's been through tings to help them see past what is glistening to them."

"Yeah man I'm trying. Some of these yutes are so disconnected from education because they don't see anyone who look like them and they don't know anyone who made it out. They need role models, man."

"That's the truth. There wasn't much when we were growing up, and it's good to see that there are organisations like roses coming through the cracks to fill gaps for these young ones."

It was good to have someone he could talk to. Ricardo silently thanked God for allowing him the chance to share without judgement. He was grateful for the moment and revelled in it.

Their conversation rode waves of previous relationships, Ricardo's current dilemma, not feeling good about himself to be a great father, movies they enjoyed, football, the Diamond League which had just past, and hobbies they possibly should have taken seriously. It was through this, Ricardo was reminded of how much he loved to be behind a camera, capturing life a frame at a time.

"When's the last time you spoke to Tony?"

"Couple weeks ago still."

"What's he up to these days?"

"Man's an engineer now, getting his ps."

"Wait he was that smart?" Stanley joked. "How did he ever get time to study? Man used to talk about how much time he spent between legs!"

"Brudda! I don't know how he finished college and went uni! We were boys but I didn't know this yute was considering uni!"

"Mad ting! Imagine, some man had it hard ah yard and you could see that on them. Then there was man like him, he had discipline, structure, support and still moved like a dickhead."

"Yo, I never thought about that you know." Ricardo's eyes shifted towards the courts, where a group of teenage boys were playing football, skins vs shirts. He wondered if that would be Jace years down the line if he didn't make a positive appearance in his son's life; skipping school to play football in the park with his friends?

"My ex, Tamara, she wants me to meet my son." His thoughts made themselves visible to Stanley. His words held a disconnect in them, they weren't cold, nor were they with any warmth. They were just words.

They lacked emotion, lacked care.

Stanley knew the statement was more to do with Ricardo questioning if he was good enough to be a father. He understood that Ricardo feared he wasn't healed enough from his past to present himself in his son's life.

"I think you should. Get to know him, spend time with him. You won't ever be fully healed so that's not even a thing to contemplate my G."

"Yeah."

"Your boy is going to need you in his life. If you're already paying child support, that's bless, but that alone can't cut it. He needs memories with you as well."

Stanley continued, telling Ricardo about some of the boys he's already come across. Boys who called their fathers sperm donors as their fathers had no physical presence in their lives. Some of the boys he met started acting out after their fathers left. Some, their fathers were in prison and left a 'legacy' for their sons to carry. Others never had their fathers in their lives and with seeing their mothers struggle, or just needing some form of structure, chose a life which was more detrimental to them.

Chapter 13: **AMENDS**

< S shayla

Dear Black Man,

I wish you never had to witness your father
projecting his insecurities on to your mother.
I wish he was taught how to value women.
I know you struggled with communicating your
differences with previous romantic partners,
but know this, you are not your father.

Think about his responses, what could he have
done better? Can you change how you wish to
respond based on what your father could have
done better? You are better than your father.
You have been healed better than he ever has
been.

I believe in you Black man. I love you.   5:32am

Letters in Black

118 Elm Tree Road
Lewisham
England
SE13 5SQ
21-Jun-2022

Dad,

I've clung to a deep hatred for you for years now. I hated the way you treated mum and as I got older and reflected on my youth, I hated you for it. I can say it was 100% easy for me to just look at you with resentment. It's another reason I cut off contact with you. With where I'm at now, I can honestly say, I am not mad at you anymore. I think I can go ahead and forgive you. Not right now, but at some point, in the future, there will be room for this to happen. I have a lot to come to terms with, I'm just rocking with the waves and tides life is giving me.

You weren't the best, that's one thing I think we can both agree on, but you taught me a lot. Some of the lessons I've learnt as I got older, but let's go for the ones I learnt as a child, as a youth.

Thank you for teaching me to appreciate life. I remember a time when you and mommy got on real good. There was no argument, everything was bless, we were happy. That was the time you briefly stopped sending me to Glen's spot. There was a Sunday we were having dinner and you looked at me and David and told us that there would come times in life, when in relationships, things would get hard and the most important thing was how we got through it together, us and our partner, not the hard times, but us actually strategising to get out of it. Now don't get me wrong, I know it wasn't something I adhered to when it came to Tamara, but, it's a good lesson. I understand it more now that I'm not with her, I'm able to look back at the bullshit I did, and know what I was meant to do to try to keep us together.

I have always been so focused on not becoming anything like you because I didn't ever want to stay with a woman and then start hitting them. As much as I never know how to properly love a Black woman, I like being with Black women, but the minute something seem like it's gonna go wrong with us, I bounce! You used to tell me and David that we shouldn't ever run from problems, and it sounds like it's a good word. However, where I was hung up on not wanting to be anything like you, that was never easy. I knew it was never right to hit a woman and mommy went through too much, I saw when her spirit broke you know. With all of that, I was like, nah, I'm not hanging around to see how things pan out with this woman because she would do shit which made me feel like I was gonna mash her up.

Your methods, to work through problems weren't right, but, what you were saying, when you actually spoke to us as your children, children you loved. Those words were everything. With all the chances I had in past to put into action what you were teaching us, I missed those marks, but it took me getting to where I'm at now to get what you meant you know.

Deep it, if shit didn't go down with Avery, nasty as that was, if I never ran off from Tamara, shit as that move was, I wouldn't have been forced to analyse myself you know. Shit needed to hit the fan for me to unlearn to relearn. I could have ended up in pen and then start thinking about things, or maybe end up dead because I'm sure man in pen don't too take kindly to man dem abusing kids.

I'm not happy about anything that I've done but I'm grateful for this shot at a second chance to make right my wrongs. I think you did teach us about how to be men whenever we would, as you so kindly put it, eff up, ha. The thing was, when you taught us that lesson, I think I lowkey dissociated, as a child, it never, nothing ever resonated, when you or Glen used to call me a man. Or say shit to pull me into manhood like, man can't be afraid of such and such, or to be a man you need to do this and that. None of that ever resonated so those lessons flew way over my head and I wasn't even tryna jump to catch them. With all of that, what I want to say is, you would say things like, when you eff up, you need to be a man about how you handle it. Accept the shit you've done wrong. Don't let pride get in the way. Own up to the shit. Find out what you can do to make sure you don't do the same shit again.

Now, with everything, I won't always get to talk to the people that I sheg up and ask them how to make sure I don't do it all again and what not, but for the people I know I can talk to, I will definitely have those conversations.

I just had to laugh to myself you know. If anyone, back in the day, try tell me that I would sit down and write a letter to you talking bout lessons you taught me, I would have laughed so hard in their face. What? Me telling you bout lessons you taught? I never used to believe there was anything positive given from you. When I say I hated you, the thought of you as my father would send venom raging through my blood and if I could have inflicted pain on you, trust me when I say, I would have done it.

I think I wanna say that I love you. I think I do dad. I think something in me believes that there is a love there for you. A love which is more directed to the times you made me feel safe you know. Those days were good.

I have to give you further credit as well. To raise a Black boy in an atmosphere which involved fear around being Black, I learnt that I belonged anywhere I went. If it wasn't for you reminding us that we were not less than anyone, and telling us that wherever our feet took us, was a space we belonged, I would never have aimed to excel in life.

Stop and searches were rife when I was younger, but because you never allowed us to dress like man dem, we stood apart and feds never looked at us too hard. I was never in crowds, I stayed to myself. I was different and that's all down to you. You made sure your boys would not be targeted.

Please accept my apology. I'm sorry for hating you. I'm sorry for never talking to you as I got older, when I got to adulthood. I should have reasoned with you, hold a meds with you. I'm sorry I allowed hatred to stop me from trying to connect with you as an adult. That volume of detest I held, told me to pull myself away from you and for that I'm sorry dad.

Bless up,

Ricky.

Letters in Black

118 Elm Tree Road
Lewisham
England
SE13 5SQ
21-Jun-2022

Ricky,

I've been asked what my future self would think of me today and I said how much I've grown. I hope when I get back to this letter later in life, I can say that I agree. Life's not been easy, it's one of those things which in hindsight you can say, it was expected. No one can ever expect that life would hand them perfection. If life was made to be perfect, there would be no balance.

It's like sun and rain. Plants can't survive on just one thing, can they? The sun is good for them, but without water, they wouldn't have all the components they need. If it was only water that they got, they would die. They need the balance and we are like plants. We need the right components to help us grow even though sometimes it's worse case scenarios, but when you extract lessons, they help to push you forward you know.

You've jumped through a lot of fire lit hoops but there are other hurdles you need to face. I want you to think about what it is you fear the most. When you think about that, think about what life would look like if that fear was sleeping. Now, when you do that, for a month, try to move in a way which defies your biggest fear right.

When you start walking bigger than your fear, think about what it is you're not doing with your life. What else is holding you back? Things like, are you holding yourself back because you aren't asking for help when you need it? Are you giving yourself the flowers you deserve? Are you running from believing in yourself, from all of the good things you can do? Things like that, I want you to think about it. When you settle on something, same again, try to work in a way which you start to do the things you're not doing. See how that impacts your future success.

You've got potential to be damn good at anything you want to do, but you need to unlock everything. Think about Naruto, man had to master chakras to release a whole lot. He had a belief so big that caused him to push and push to get closer to his goal. No matter how hard it ever got for him, he would always fight to be better, find other ways to do what needed to be done. Now I'm not saying you're an anime character, but I'm saying, there are lessons to rock out with. As well as that, you need to find a motivating factor, you know, like Sasuke was for Naruto.

Pull lessons from the things you read, the movies you watch, the animes you watch. Find the lessons between the lines, and apply them to your life. Reflect on you, what you've done, what you want to do, what's holding you back, what life would be like if these things weren't holding you back. Use that to propel you.

Big love to you my guy.

Bless up.

Ricky.

Letters in Black

118 Elm Tree Road
Lewisham
England
SE13 5SQ
21-Jun-2022

Dear Jace,

Son, I'm sorry for any pain I've caused you. I don't know when I'll hand this letter to you, but you will definitely be someone who gets one of these letters I've written. I didn't have the best childhood, but I had a childhood. I didn't have the best father, but I had a father. I would love to think that I'm active in your life as your father, which is why I know you'll get this.

Your mum wanted me to get to know you and while I'm trying to figure things out right now, I know I will come round to getting to know you. Even though I left your mother while she was pregnant, I was sending her money to get ready for your birth. I carried on sending money to help out, same amount that would be required as child support and a bit more just because you're worth more than child support allowances. The one thing I was never ready to do though, was get to know you because I was hard on myself.

I reprimanded myself a lot and even thought that I needed to get to a point of perfection before I could be present. I guess I was also scared to give you mixed signals by being around but causing you more grievance you know. Don't get me wrong, you're going to find that from time to time, you will get mad at me, not understanding why I do or say what I say, but I guarantee you one thing, as you get older, it will all start to click and then you'll be like raa that's what dad was saying.

I want you to enjoy your childhood, be a little boy, then be a preteen boy, then be a teen-aged boy, then an adolescent before becoming a man. If I've ever made you feel like you need to grow up quicker than you should and I say anything which resembles a need to be a man, forgive me. Take your time to forgive me though, you need to understand what it is you're forgiving me for. This may come in adulthood, but, please forgive me.

You will at times need to revisit your youth in order to work with your inner child to give him freedom to reign in you. You might get this letter while you're young so it won't mean a lot to you, but reread it frequently, just to refresh your memory, remind you of what I've said.

I want you to analyse my actions, pick it apart, if it helps, talk me through how my actions affect you. Talk to me about how what I've done doesn't sit well with you. Don't ever tiptoe around these subjects. As my son, an unintentional carrier of my problems, I want you to come to me and let's discuss it. I'm working on myself to become open to these discussions with you so I don't clam up and become defensive when you want to have these conversations.

I love you and I want the best for you. The world can be a cruel place and I don't want to force you to not have a safe space, so I'm working on becoming that. Thank you for teaching me lessons I need to help assist you in this life.

I love you son.

Dad.

Letters in Black

118 Elm Tree Road
Lewisham
England
SE13 5SQ
21-Jun-2022

Tamara,

I wish I knew how to love you the way you deserved to be loved. I wish I knew how to be a man who was clued up on how to trust; I should have trusted you with my past and that you would have made the best choice. I'm sorry I stole that moment from you. I think that was the most selfish thing I did during our relationship.

I would love to believe we had a good time while we were together, despite me hiding pieces of me from you. I guess I can say my biggest downfall was the fact that I didn't create room for a proper friendship with you. What I mean is, I've learnt something from my friendship with Shayla, I removed my mask with her. I'm honest enough for her to see what it looks like when I get in my head and allow my insecurities to change me.

When I was with you, I was always holding myself back, trying to be someone I wasn't because I didn't know how to be me with you when all the thoughts became surface demons. I became a puppet you know. Like, it governed my life in such a way I didn't even realise how much of me I was hiding. Those things would pop up and make me feel inadequate next to you, but still, there is a cloak I would wear, harden myself, became the best actor I could to make things seem like they were okay.

Want to know what broke me? The day you told me that I was perfect. It was two days after I met Shayla, I was telling you about her and how she caught me slippin. You didn't think I needed to read self-help books, but she found it admirable that a Black man would show strangers that he was interested in bettering himself.

I've been learning to forgive myself over the past couple months, more so this past month and I have to say, I'm struggling with forgiving myself for having you feel that I was some kind of killer. I can't forget the look of fear crawling over your skin, you froze, I remember how heavy your feet got in my hands. It was hard for me to really see my girlfriend in front of me. Your demeanour changed drastically in a short time frame and you asked me how many people I bodied. Even though I laughed in the moment, it hurt me a hell of a lot afterwards.

You know what the maddest thing is, even though you were pregnant, I didn't even think to check in on you, see how you were doing. All I wanted to do from then was to stay far from you, you know. I thought that's what was best for you, but you could have gotten so stressed that it would cause complications with the pregnancy, but that was far from being a thought of mine.

I'm sorry for my selfishness.

I want to hope that one day you will be able to find it in your heart to forgive me. Some may say I'm not worth being forgiven. Your mum, I can imagine her telling you that she already told you from the jump that I was wuklis and good for nothing. Can't lie, that me, definitely, he was a big wuklis man. He didn't know better and it's taken up to now for me to even own up to my shit. Not that I ever blamed you for anything, it was never your fault. I think you are the first female I got into anything with and I never pinned blame on you. I think there's a part of me that fell in love with you and that all taught me to chill. I was wrong, didn't acknowledge it fully, but I never blamed you.

I'm sure you've been a fantastic mother to Jace. Thank you for keeping the name. I don't deserve a huge place in his life after what I've done, but you would like me to meet my son, become a part of his life, so thank you. Thanks for believing that I'm worth being a part of his life. I hope to be what he needs in a father. Please step in if you feel there is something I'm doing which is of detriment to him, but also please trust that I've gained the knowledge and experience to protect him as best as possible.

You are an exceptional woman. I wish I knew and recognised this sooner. You deserve a man who sees this in you the minute he gets to know you.

That's it from me.

Ricky.

The breath he released seemed to have been caught in his chest throughout the three letters he wrote. As he brought himself back to his surroundings, he could hear rustling outside his door, bags, held in the hands of one of his neighbours as they walked by. He could hear faint chatter, the voices sounding similar to Miles and Janet. The sun that spilled into his living room seemed to be brighter today, strong enough to come with a message for him.

He placed the book he had been leaning on to the left of him. The letters, yet to be placed in envelopes, looked up at him, pleading to remain in the open. They wanted to feel freedom dance along their lines, weaving between each letter as they formed connections to become words. Ricardo closed his eyes and stretched the kinks out of his body, giving each letter their request. Granting them their wish.

What would it have been like if two years ago I was arrested and charged? Ricardo pondered. This was that thought he never gave opportunity to loiter for too long. He was never strong enough to handle the remnants of what was, to think about what could have been. He had a complacency kept within the realms of knowing that nothing happened, his safe haven.

What would it have been like if two years ago I was arrested and charged? The thought pressed him, more urgency in its presence. He sat carefully with it as it grew, trying to find an answer. Could this be the thing he wrote in his letter, the fear he had? Was it a fear of knowing that other possibility which stopped him answering, well, entertaining this question previously?

Taking slow deep breaths, drinking in the stream of the sun's rays, he made room in his psyche for the possibility to show itself. *I wouldn't have been who I am now.* The answer he was looking for but always scared to give himself. To know he could never be this version of who he was, one he was becoming comfortable with, was what he couldn't accept. The truth.

Another shot at being in my son's life would have never been on the table, and my job, of course I would have lost that. In comparison to a white man who may have been in as a serial paedophile or something, I can bet my sentence would have been longer than his. Bringing himself to his feet, Ricardo made his way to the kitchen. Big thoughts needed coffee. To succumb to a thought that has always threatened to plague his mind, at 8am, his mind needed to be fuelled.

"Alexa play T-Pain Three Rings album" his voice travelled. He heaped a teaspoon with coffee granules before dumping it into his 'I'm too depressed for this shit' mug, poured a small amount of hot water and stirred. Pausing for a brief moment, he contemplated a strictly black coffee with no sugar, but like his mug, he decided he was too depressed and chose to add oat milk and sugar.

It felt good to be alive once more. To know there was something he could look forward to, smiles he could hope to see, it felt good. As T-Pains' sounds poured through his speaker, Ricardo bopped his head to the beat, allowed his body to reconfigure as each fibre reconnected with what it felt like to move freely.

Dance, the ultimate form of freedom. The way a body would move through time, guided by inner peace, the need to shed what no longer served purpose. The way a body could defy the need to answer questions. Dance caused an individual to shed their worries. It wasn't a need of entertainment, it was a way to bond with their subconscious and create openings, bubbles of joy.

Chapter 14: **PUSH**

Friday, 24 June

Dear Black Man,

It's been a rough number of months, but you've done very well. You have not compromised your healing and you've managed to revise your circle of friends. I know it wasn't an easy thing to do, but on your journey to healing, you knew the decision that would be best for you.

Love you Black Man

5:32am

Letters in Black

118 Elm Tree Road
Lewisham
England
SE13 5SQ
24-Jun-2022

To the man I am today.

Shayla's right. You have done better than you've really given yourself credit for. You've spent so much time, and energy, as of late, trying to figure out the pieces of your life which wasn't the greatest, yet you've not acknowledged the greatness within you.

This world was not created to assist Black men and I'm sure I don't even need to go into where it started. It's a cold world, but you kept the flame within you burning and held on to its warmth. That's what kept you going. you didn't just survive, but you allowed yourself to come through the cracks in your life to be who you are now. The key to growth isn't hidden in books, it's instead locked away in the corners of the human mind and reveals itself when one's down to their last thread.

You are more than just text messages received in the morning and a world more than family members hating you for your mistakes. I want to say that the issue is, you kept trying to present a fallacy and that's what led to your downfall. That's what I want to say, but I think the truth is that, if it wasn't for those fallacies, for the hidden truths from Chloe, you wouldn't have been in the position to go face to face with the past. Having never been taught how to approach your Goliaths, you fed them, you watered them and then they became too much for you to handle. It's not your fault, it's not even your parents' fault. The man you were in 2019 is thankful for it all. You have a world filled with stars waiting for you to catch them as they fall, all because you endured.

I'm proud of you for hanging in there man. Remember, this is only the beginning my guy.

There are going to be futures with the past as a loitering ghost wanting your downfall to happen. Just remember that you overcame once and will be able to do it again and again.

Don't watch what other man's doing. Forgive mommy. She has a whole other story you may never know, but forgive her. You can try with her again, same way you approached Niyah to forgive you, try approach mommy and try forgive her. There is room in your heart for it. Don't be a mule and walk with a dagger in your heart. That's just big-time hypocrisy fam.

And he's dead. Glen is dead. His story you will never get unless someone willingly offers it up. Don't worry about digging up old bones. You are nothing like him. I want you to work on erasing the bridge you drew between both of your lives. Don't downplay what you've been through. Like the choir boys mentioned in the news who were molested by priests, like the actors who were molested by directors, your story is important. It's important for you to ac-knowledge because it affected your choices. Don't downplay it because you need to remember the importance in protecting your son.

The protection you didn't get as a kid, give it to him. When you see Tamara later, rebuild a bond with her and discuss this notion with her again. It's something you tried in the past but you was hella cryptic. When you see her, remember, she knows what happened, so discuss this with her. It's a conversation bigger than couple hours sitting down in a restaurant talking or in a park. Do you even know where you two are going yet? What would you do if... nah I'm not even going there.

Fun and games aside, you have a lifetime a head of you with a little life line who needs to learn to communicate with your and his mother. When you begin to make appearances in his life, create a safe space for him and with him so he trusts you as he grows, to stay truthful to you.

Letters in Black

Fathers are to be figures of safety, but it's a dismissed concept because, man ain't meant to be emotional. Imagine, we're humans right, men are meant to be humans, but yet still we ain't meant to be emotional. How the hell does that even make sense? What does showing emotions have to do with being, or creating a safe space? But, talking about emotions, stay in touch with yourself bredrin. It's needed. Show your emotions with those who you cross paths with. If you're upset, let it be known, don't walk round and act like say everything is kriss. I'm not saying every day you're out there bawling down the place, but, be human and not a piece of board. All of that to say, the way you feel, is valid.

Be bold in being honest to yourself and those who love you. You are loved.

Bless up King!

As he finished with writing his letter, Ricardo felt the pulse from his heart pounding through his chest. He closed his eyes and listened to the steady thud; a drum beat. It was the drummer, keeping the rhythm of his life. Cool air tickled the thin hair in his nostrils as it snuck in to travel to his lungs. He held his breath as gases settled in his lungs sorting themselves out, one set waiting to be exhaled whilst newly inhaled made their way to the manager for guidance. The exhale felt better. He felt his muscles lightened as their load was released.

An alarm he set on his phone proudly announced itself to remind him that it was time to start getting ready. He and Tamara agreed on a date to spend some time together. He had never chased butterflies in his childhood, but here he was, an adult, fearing the flutter of their wings in his stomach. It wasn't the day for him to meet Jace, but it was the start of a future he never once looked forward to having left.

The invasive thoughts opened doors of insecurities, screaming at him. Ricardo laughed as they attempted to keep him down. This was not an opportunity he was going to allow to slip through his fingers. Now more than ever, he was going to be what he didn't have as a child. He was going to make every effort to right some wrongs.

He had no idea what Tamara had in mind, just that it was a chill thing so went for a pair of blue jeans, his blue and white Jordans, a white t-shirt and a blue and white varsity jacket. He mulled over the thought of a snapback, putting it on and taking it off repeatedly. Not able to decide what to do, he took a selfie and sent a picture to Shayla asking her opinion.

Get a grip of yourself fool. Giving himself a once over, he pulled his jacket, popped his head back slightly and licked his lips. It was college all over again. Getting ready for a date, had to make certain that he looked right. His reflection would show him the smize he needed, or the way to curl his lips, or, the right way to bite his bottom lip with the devious look beneath his lids. They were going to go to Mountsfield Park with a group of friends. They weren't exclusive and with the lack of individuality amongst them, it was easy for them to spend a lot of their time together, with their group of friends. It was very rare that they were alone, and when they were, they were more like adults than teenagers.

The train into Victoria was an okay ride, but getting on the Circle Line to High Street Kensington was a nightmare. The Circle Line was to be one of the nicer underground trains in London, but, at this time of year where schools in other countries were already on summer break, families poured onto the train with him at Victoria. *It's only four stops,* he repeated to himself.

There was a Black family opposite him, a little boy roughly Jace's age, asking his dad questions about other commuters, "why does that man have pink hair?", "why did we have to take the train?", "why does that woman have a dog on the train? The train isn't a park". Ricardo smiled to himself. He imagined being in the position of the dad, thinking about what he would have said to Jace. Was the answer the child received more important or was it more important to interact with them despite the answers? He acknowledged the family with a smile before stepping off the train.

This was it. Today he got to spend time with his past love, the mother of his child. His heart thudded a little harder in his chest. His track record with the women in his family was not the greatest so he hoped that this would be a better kind of day. That's all he could do.

He tried to read the person in front of him, her physique, her eyes, her face, her hand gestures. Futile as it was, he tried to understand her. He wanted to know how Tamara felt about him. She had every right to hate him if she did. If she were to slap him, in public, shame would leave his side and expose him to onlookers as the man who left his pregnant girlfriend.

Ricardo wanted to reach out to her, take her hands in his, feel her spindly fingers in his hands. She was off limits. There was a moat around her, she allowed him an appointment slot to see her, to talk to her, but not touch her, not feel her in his arms. The memories of how she felt when encased in his arms screamed loudly in his mind. Their ghosts provoked his inner darkness to the surface, all in hopes to engulf him.

His eyes followed hers as they fell on her hands holding an invisible pencil, doodling away on the table. She kept her fingers busy as though they missed threading needles and guiding fabric through sewing machines. He imagined she was guiding remnants of their past through a machine, stitching all the pieces together that they would make sense, if any could be brought out from what he created.

This was not what he was expecting. Tamara wasn't fully opposed to Shayla, but she was sceptical in the beginning. Shayla understood boundaries and had never pushed Ricardo into thinking of her in anyway other than as a friend, the random stranger on the train turned friend.

"It never use" – her voice broke into the silence, trembling "are you still in touch with Shayla?" Eyes still fixated on her hands running things through the machine.

"Yeah, we talk ever so often."

"No relationship on the horizon?"

"Huh?"

"You liked her, and if you're still in touch with her it means you didn't push her away as you did me, so, is there a relationship with her on the horizon?"

Tamara raced through her words with rough patches in her breathing, but she held it together. Ambushing Ricardo with her choice of words, like daggers, if thrown with accuracy, would hit the nerves connected to his pain receptors. Tamara saw what Tony saw, yet Ricardo failed to understand it.

"Nothing's there."

"She still sending those texts?"

Her beautiful brown eyes now piercing his. The halo around her iris calling out for his honesty.

"Yeah. Some of them have been thought provocative."

"She likes you."

"Why can't it just be a platonic thing? She sees a friend in need of healing and she is being supportive."

"If it makes you sleep at night believing that's the case, I'll drop it." Her laugh was soft, it was calm. Her face melted at the warmth she radiated, her pages being shown, there was legibility now.

"God gifted you with her at the right time though. He knew things were going to blow up and you'd run. You needed someone new who you could lean on without worrying they'd judge you. I'm glad you had her."

"Thanks."

There was no change in her. She remained the same, kind hearted, understanding woman she's always been, despite the pain she felt.

"I'm learning a lot you know. Like, what I owe myself and what I don't owe to anyone else. I wouldn't have imagined my life burning the way it did, but if it didn't happen, things would have gotten worse in a different way."

The moment felt right. It felt easy and Ricardo wanted to keep it that way. He would have loved to have it that way, but, guilt in the pit of his stomach like coal in a jerk pan seemed to have found its ignition fluid, the smoke awakening followed by fire. It was no easy feat to make amends to a past life, with a past lover, while growing to be a better person. It felt wrong to move past all the damage he caused without her, the woman he hurt, and their son, by his side for them to all grow together.

"I hope it doesn't sound selfish of me, but thank you for not chasing me when I left. I think I would have caved, come back to you and acted stupidly ungodly and things would have been worse." He returned her smile. "Also, thanks for never trying to force me out of a friendship with Shayla. You're right, I needed her to survive. She was still a stranger, but I needed that, someone I could have lost if I opened up, without fear of losing her."

THE END

Dear Black Men,

Society has not been easy on you, but you've done exceptionally well to survive the betrayal you've faced. You've inherited years of hatred from all parties, but you've been exceedingly resilient. With your tenacity, I doubt the White men from our history lessons would have been fearful. I would like to applaud you, Black man.

If you are battling with trauma, Black man, please, seek out a therapist. This is for your own good. If you have no one you can turn to, seek out a therapist. It's important that you speak to someone instead of hanging on to years of trauma that will eat away at you. You are precious and valuable. I need you to survive.

To the Black man who still has night tremors. To the Black man who has demons showing their face to him. To the Black man who was molested and was never able to speak. I love you. On behalf of those who harmed you, I'm sorry. Be patient with yourself. Speak kindly to the King within. You are healing, and it shows. I love you, Black man.

From a Black woman who won't beat you down.
With love,
Careen Latoya Lawrence.

To my readers,

For those of you who are returning, I would like to say thank you for your continued support. If you are new to the world of Careen Latoya, hey! Welcome to the club. I hope to see you again for the next release.

Thank you all for reading. I'm assuming you're now reading this as you've made it through the book. It's that, or you chose to read the end of the book first. Please know, I truly appreciate you, don't forget that.

I write not only for myself but for you also. I am most thankful that you all allow me to continue on this path.

I understand that this may not have been the easiest of reads, and you getting to the end means the world to me. It definitely wasn't an easy write for me. While writing, I'd see videos of men saying something absurd, making me question if I should continue writing. I also observed how I saw men treating women, which made me sick to my stomach. That said, I had to remember the men I was writing about.

The research I did around this topic before writing weighed heavy on me. One thing I used as a form of research, though they weren't voices of Black men, was watching videos on Youtube by Soft White Underbelly. Those stories were heavy. I watched a lot of The Terrell Show, also on Netflix, followed by Naruto over on Crunchyroll to push through.

As I said before, this was not an easy project for me. I needed motivators to help me to make it through. I say all of that to say I understand wholeheartedly how difficult a read it would have been for you. With that, I can't express how grateful I am to you for making your way to the end. This is also the reason I suggested the playlist at the beginning. Something to get you through the read to give you the balance you needed.

Oh and just to let you know, the final book in this trilogy will be 'Healing In Black'. I would love to give you an approximate release date, but I would be setting us both up for a disappointment in the event it doesn't happen on that date. In the meantime, keep up with me over on Instagram @careen_latoya. Facebook and TikTok are also used by me, but not much, so Instagram is the safest bet.

Love you all.
Careen Latoya Lawrence.

The Home of Careen Latoya
Eastbourne
Tuesday 9th August 2022

Personal Thank Yous,

Firstly, I would like to say a huge thank you to Dawnshaeé for starting the Introtoeclecticm Book Club! It's a virtual book club, and I learned about Wahala by Nikki May through the group. It was our February read, and that particular book held me. By the end of the book, I decided there was a character I despised. As a result, it led to my theory that if you get to the end of a book and there's a character you can't stand, it's an indicator of a great book.

This leads to my second thank you, Lucrecia Seline. Had it not been for our conversation about that book and you allowing me to ramble on, we would have never thought about the antagonist in Love in Black. Thank you for that particular conversation. Had you not suggested that I tell Ricardo's story, book 4 would have potentially had been a book of poems.

My third thank you goes to those who completed the questionnaires I created. Your feedback is the reason Ricardo didn't end up behind bars as I initially wanted to happen when I thought about telling his story.

My third thank you goes to three men, Spades Lunn, Solomon Adams and Benna Waite. I got to a point where I was unsure of a particular section I wrote, and these men were kind enough to allow me to send that sample to them so they could give me feedback.

To the Black Booktokers, you are all so amazing. I don't follow many of you, but those I follow, particularly Robin - Sometimesrobinreads, your reviews on other books helped me big time!

My final thank you goes to my Beta Readers, Patrick, Charnjit and Robin, your reviews were everything! Honestly, your feedback helped the final shape of this book. You are all amazing. Thank you for your honesty. Thank you for taking the time out for this book.

Love you all.
Careen Latoya Lawrence.

Other books by Careen Latoya Lawrence

Free (2015)
Naked Lenses (2017)
Love in Black (2021)

Books prepared for publishing by Careen Latoya Lawrence

Cora & The Power of 5 by Rhae'nell K Allen (2021)
It Will Be: The Black Experience - poetry anthology (2021)
You are Seen, You are Heard, You are Loved by Akeem Lloyd (2022)

Milton Keynes UK
Ingram Content Group UK Ltd.
UKHW010645120124
435917UK00004B/276